Lisa

A GRAND MAN

Catherine Cookson was born in East Jarrow and the place of her birth provides the background she so vividly creates in many of her novels. Although acclaimed as a regional writer – her novel THE ROUND TOWER won the Winifred Holtby Award for the best regional novel of 1968 – her readership spreads throughout the world. Her work has been translated into twelve languages and Corgi alone has over 20,000,000 copies of her novels in print, including those written under the name of Catherine Marchant.

Mrs Cookson was born the illegitimate daughter of a poverty-stricken woman, Kate, whom she believed to be her older sister. Catherine began work in service but eventually moved South to Hastings where she met and married a local grammar school master. At the age of forty she began writing with great success about the lives of the working-class people of the North-East with whom she had grown up, including her intriguing autobiography, OUR KATE. More recently THE CINDER PATH has established her position as one of the most popular of contemporary women novelists.

Mrs Cookson now lives in Northumberland, overlooking the Tyne.

D0711047

Catherine Cookson

A Grand Man

CORGI BOOKS
A DIVISION OF TRANSWORLD PUBLISHERS LTD

A GRAND MAN
A CORGI BOOK 0 552 08821 8

Originally published in Great Britain
by Macdonald & Co. (Publishers) Ltd.

PRINTING HISTORY
Macdonald edition published 1954
Corgi edition published 1971
Corgi edition reprinted 1972
Corgi edition reprinted 1973
Corgi edition reprinted 1974
Corgi edition reprinted 1976
Corgi edition reprinted 1977
Corgi edition reprinted 1978
Corgi edition reprinted 1979 (twice)
Corgi edition reprinted 1980
Corgi edition reprinted 1981

Everything in this story is fictitious, except that which
you yourself know to be true.

This book is set in Intertype Baskerville

Corgi Books are published by Transworld Publishers Ltd.,
Century House, 61–63 Uxbridge Road,
Ealing, London W5 5SA
Printed and bound in Great Britain by
Hunt Barnard Printing Ltd., Aylesbury, Bucks.

CONTENTS

CHAPTER ONE

A BIT OF IMAGINATION

In the quiet corner of the school yard Mary Ann stood surrounded by a little band of open-mouthed, silent admirers. With waving movements of her thin arms she drew them closer about her, and when they were pressed near she warmed to her theme.

'And besides the great big house,' she said, her eyes moving from one to the other, like revolving saucers, 'we've got three servants and two cars and two horses ... galloping ones.' She curved her arms into what she considered was the shape of the horses legs, and she jerked them at a great speed to indicate the velocity of the steeds. 'And,' she finished in a voice weighed with awe, 'some day I'll show you them; and our house, and the car besides, some day when I have a party.'

The children stared at her in admiration. Then one after the other they put forth tentative offers that might act as a sprat to catch a mackerel.

'Would you like a stot of me ball, Mary Ann?'

'I'll lend you me thick skipping rope at the week-end, Mary Ann.'

'When I spent me penny on Saturda' I'll save you some, Mary Ann.'

Whether Mary Ann would have accepted any of these offers cannot be known, for at that moment an indignant figure came rushing round the corner of the school wall and startled them all by crying, 'Oh, you big liar, Mary Ann Shaughnessy! I've been listening behind the wall. You don't live in a big house, and you ain't got no servants or cars or horses. Oh, was there ever such a liar as you?'

The little crowd turned its eyes from the black-haired, vicious-faced accuser back to Mary Ann, and expectantly awaited developments.

Mary Ann felt no immediate anger against her enemy ... Sarah Flannagan was always spoiling people's fun. And anyway, it wasn't lies she was telling, it was more in the nature of a story. Yes, that was it. This soothed her conscience, but she couldn't tell them that it was just a story. No, oh no. She felt a sudden spasm of pity for them; they had listened to her so intently – they were the best lot she had talked to for a long time. Looking back into the eyes of her audience, she realized that she owed them something, a show of defence at any rate. So she cocked her elfin face on one side and blinked her large brown eyes at Sarah Flannagan, and said quite calmly, 'You know nothing whatever about our house, or me da's car, Sarah Flannagan; and I'll thank you to mind your own business.' She nodded at the children, and the nod said, 'There, that's settled her hash.'

The dark spoiler of dreams gasped, and for a moment was struck speechless; then sucking in her lips and making a sound that was a good imitation of frying bacon, she turned to the eager group, her head wagging as quickly as her tongue as she cried, 'Why! of all the whopping liars she's one. She lives right opposite us; and not in a house like ours either, but in Mulhattans' Hall. They've only got two wee rooms and a cupboard of a kitchen. And as for her da having a car ... why! my! huh! He can't even keep down a job 'cause he's always on the booze.'

Knowing she had played her trump card, Sarah Flannagan's vituperation ceased, but her chin, thrust out towards the slight, quivering figure of Mary Ann, was defying her to get over that shattering piece of integrity.

Now the poised calm of Mary Ann had vanished, and her eyes were blazing with an anger that lent to her little frame the energy of lightning. She almost sprang on the indignant stickler for truth, stopped only, it would seem, by the jutting chin of her enemy. Her voice shaking with an emotion that could only be classed as uncontrollable rage, she shouted, 'You! you pig face! you wicked thing. I'll slap your face, so I will, if you dare say me da drinks. Oh . . . h!' She cast her eyes heavenwards. 'It's a wonder God doesn't strike you down dead. But you'll go to hell for your wickedness . . . Oh, yes you will.' She pointed an accusing finger, and had only to add 'I'll see to it' to give the stamp of absolute authority to this last statement.

Sarah Flannagan was not in the least intimidated by this threat to her future, but turned her fishy eyes on to the group that had widened and spread itself away from Mary Ann.

Mary Ann too looked at her late admirers, and beseechingly she entreated them, 'Don't believe a word she says. My da's a lovely man. He gets sick at times but he never drinks. And he tells the loveliest stories. Look, some day I'll take you . . . home. . . .'

The words trailed away as Sarah Flannagan laughed: 'She thinks she's safe with you lot that comes from the Fifteen Streets; she doesn't tell them lies to anybody living round our way.'

The faces, whose attention Mary Ann had held so eagerly a few minutes ago, now looked at her in silence and condemnation, for to partake in the make-believe world of childhood is not to lie unless the word lie is actually uttered, but once it is then make-believe is wrong; it immediately becomes a sin – another weight to be carried on the head until the priest removes it in confession; lies were connected

9

with penance and purgatory. Mary Ann Shaughnessy had been found out.

With one accord they backed away. Then turning together like pigeons in flight, they went hitching and skipping around the personification of truth as she walked triumphantly out of the school yard with a backward leer to where Mary Ann stood with trembling lips and the burning sting of tears in the backs of her eyes.

The blazing indignation had died out of her as quickly as it had arisen, and after waiting in order to give her tormentor a good start, she too walked out of the yard and made her way home. And to comfort herself, she decided that if she could cover the whole distance homewards without once stepping on a crack in the pavement any wish she might make would be bound to come true.

To this end she began a series of hops, jumps and long and short strides, of stepping into the gutter when confronted by a paving stone so cracked that it was impossible to hop, jump or stride over it. It was when confronted by such a stretch of pavement that she was knocked right into the middle of it by two boys rushing out of Stanley Street. Their wild stampede carried her before them and left her staring down at her feet lying bang across a crack.

Her face worked and her lips trembled, and she could have cried with vexation. She had so wanted a wish, just another wish to make doubly sure of the week-end. She couldn't have too many wishes to ... keep the week-end right. And the week-end started tonight, because it was Friday night and her da got his pay packet the night. She stood uncertain for a moment, plucking at her lip. Then her face brightened and she hopped clean off the diseased pavement on to a whole but greasy slab. She knew what she would do; she'd go and have a talk with The Holy Family. If anybody could make sure of the week-end, they could.

This decision made, she hurried back along the main road,

charitably forgetful of the times when the Holy Family had slipped up in their duty and the week-ends had been a failure.

As she neared the church, its external severity filled her with nothing but hope and its interior gaudiness lifted her heart and clothed her with peace.

Going up to the small side altar she knelt down below the life-size statues of the Virgin, with the Child in her arms, and St. Joseph standing protectingly near. She gazed up at them for some moments in silence before beginning her routine. First she blessed herself; then she lifted the Sacred Heart Medal that was reposing on her chest at the end of a narrow brass chain, which she would have assured you was solid gold, and she laid this on the front of her coat so that it would not escape the notice of the influential ones. Then bringing to her face what she called her 'good look', she said, in a voice that was a mixture of Tyneside and Irish, 'Oh, Holy Family, I've come to ask you something; and I'll do anything you like for you if you'll grant my request.'

She waited, as if to let her offer sink in, before going on, 'I want you to keep me da from being sick at the week-end, 'cause he's a lovely da, as you know, and he doesn't mean to make me ma cry. He told her so last night himself when he thought I was asleep in bed. He told her it was sorry he was to the heart, and if only we could all get back into the country he'd give up the ... I mean he wouldn't be sick any more; it's having to work in the shipyard and them factories that makes him want to be sick. And there's nothing but yards round here to work in. But mind,' she put in, hastily, 'I'm not blaming you for making so many yards; you've had to put them some place.' She nodded, expressing her sympathy at what must have been a dilemma to them.

Then she went on, 'But you see, me da doesn't like them; he likes the country. And he won't go into it to work without me ma and me and our Michael. And that's where the cottage comes in. You'll mind I asked you about it last week. If only you could see your way clear to getting us a cottage, just a little weeny one would do, I'd do anything for you, Jesus, Mary and Joseph. I'll even stop telling lies about the servants and the horses. I will, honest to God.'

She had a vague idea that something should happen at this point, a clapping of hands at least. She gazed up at the group of statuary in strained, expectant silence, and had to be content when the infant child looked up at his mother with a 'Well, what about it?' look on his face.

The Virgin must have taken the cue, for quite suddenly Mary Ann experienced a feeling of relief, and tears, which she was sure she had not started, ran down her cheeks, and she was powerless to stop them.

She blessed herself, and having risen, she genuflected deeply; then turned away and walked almost into the arms of Father Owen.

The old priest, with his bald head and long solemn face, hung over her for a moment and affected astonishment at seeing her. He made not the smallest reference to her tear-stained face, but he bent down and whispered, 'You've a great devotion to the Holy Family, I notice, Mary Ann.'

Blinking, smiling and sniffing, all in one movement, she whispered back confidentially, 'Yes, Father, 'cause it's nearly the same size as our family.'

'Oh, of course. Yes, yes,' he nodded at her. 'You're a good girl.' He patted her cheek, and the smile left her face and her head drooped, and she took small, quiet steps on her toes up the aisle, the priest walking as noiselessly by her side.

When she whispered something that he could not catch, he bent his long frame towards her, asking, 'What is it?' And she, still with eyes averted, whispered, 'I'm not a good girl, Father, I'm a howling liar.'

The priest's eyebrows moved slightly, and he said, 'Oh, indeed?'

And Mary Ann nodded to the heating grid over which she stepped carefully, and said, 'Yes.'

In silence they reached the end of the church and came to a halt where the holy water font was attached to a pillar. Mary Ann dipped in her fingers and once again blessed herself, and the priest, standing looking at her, sighed and exclaimed, 'Ah well. It's a good thing when we know what we are, but I think you're too hard on yourself. That's a bit too strong a name for you, Mary Ann.'

'It isn't, Father. Oh, it isn't,' she whispered emphatically.

She had called herself a howling liar, and the priest must take her word that that was what she was; he mustn't take things lightly like this. She stretched up to him and went on to explain, still in a whisper, 'You see, Father, I tell people we've got cars and horses and servants, and we haven't.'

'Oh, you do?' The priest's eyebrows moved again.

'Yes.'

'Dear, dear. Cars, horses and servants?'

'Yes.'

They stared at each other.

'Well, well; this is serious. They couldn't be just nice day-dreams you've been having?'

'No, oh no, Father.'

'Dear, dear me. Cars, horses and servants. What are we going to do about it?'

'I've talked to the Holy Family, Father.'

'You have?'

'Yes, Father. And I promised them I won't lie again. And I meant to promise them I won't get into any more rages either, but. . . .'

'Do you get into rages, Mary Ann?'

'I do, Father; when anybody says me da . . .' She hesitated

and her eyes drooped once more, and she toyed with her hair ribbon which was hanging perilously on the end of one plait.

'Yes, Mary Ann,' prompted Father Owen. 'And what do they say?'

'Well' – she looked straight up into the priest's eyes – 'people say me da drinks; and you know yourself, Father, he doesn't. You know he never touches a drop.'

The child and the priest regarded each other intently; and as Mary Ann watched the priest's nostrils quiver and his right eyebrow jerk spasmodically, very like the head of Mr. Lavey, who lived on the ground floor of their house and who had the tick, she felt forced to press her point again.

'He might get sick now and then, but he doesn't drink. Does he, Father?'

The appeal in the great eyes, the strain visible in the thin wisp of a body, did not touch the priest as much as did the unseen but evident conflict of loyalties raging in the heart of this child who had the art of conjuring up and of living numbers of separate lives, each with the same focal point, her father . . . and him a drunken agitator, and not of the faith either! Which, in a way, was something to be thankful for. No, no – he chided himself for his thoughts – it could be the saving of him if he'd come in. . . .

'Does he, Father?' The whispered insistence made him pinch his quivering nose between his finger and thumb, and with a sliding glance at the cross hanging above the holy water font, he said, almost defiantly, 'Not a drop, Mary Ann. Not a drop. I know that.'

Mary Ann sighed, and she smiled, and her young mouth stretched wide in happiness as she said, 'I knew you would speak the truth, Father.'

Her pleasure, however, turned to immediate concern when she saw her dear, dear Father Owen almost choke.

Something must have stuck in his throat, for he was going red in the face with coughing.

Still coughing, the priest led Mary Ann to the door, and patting her head, he nodded to her in farewell, for he was unable to speak.

In grave concern, Mary Ann watched him re-enter the church. Poor Father Owen; he had a bad cold. Eeh . . . the thought swept over her making her hot . . . what if he were to get the 'flu and die? Oh, but he wouldn't. God wouldn't let Father Owen die. She could not see the Creator being such a cold-blooded monster as to take away her confidant, friend, and what was more, her ally in defence of her father.

Suddenly she skipped off the church step. Wouldn't that be one in the eye for Sarah Flannagan when she told her what Father Owen had said? 'Sarah Flannagan,' she would say to her, 'now shut your big gob and listen to this. Father Owen said . . . and mind he was standing near the holy water font and the cross above him when he said it, and not even you'll dare to say Father Owen tells lies. . . . Well, standing there, he said, "I've never known your da to touch a drop of drink, Mary Ann. And anybody that says it will go to Hell and be shrivelled up." So there!' By, that would be like a slap across her nasty big face.

For the moment she felt very happy. Father Owen was the bestest man in the world, next to her da. Eeh. Well, was her da better than the priest?

She spent most of the time that it took her to reach home in debating in which position of goodness she should place the two men who were a power in her life.

CHAPTER TWO

MULHATTANS' HALL

MULHATTANS' HALL was a small tenement house jammed between two-storey houses consisting of two rooms upstairs and two down. In any other part of the country these would have been termed flats, but in Jarrow and the surrounding towns two rooms so placed was called a house, and if, as sometimes happened, the back-yard had been designed that each occupant had a slit of private concrete with a high wall cutting him off from his near neighbour, then that occupant had a right to feel that he was socially on the upgrade. It can therefore be guessed how far down the social scale were the five families living in Mulhattans' Hall, for here there was only one communal back-yard, and from it water for all uses had to be carried.

The official name of Mulhattans' Hall was sixteen Burton Street. It had come by its title from a family of that name who had lived there some years before, and from occupying one 'house' the family, through marriage, had spread into the other four parts; and since they were all sons who had married the house had become a hive of Mulhattans, and far from a peaceful hive; and although the last of these Mulhattans had long since gone the name still remained.

Five families still occupied the Hall; the Shaughnessys on the attic floor, Miss Harper and the Quigleys on the first floor, and on the ground floor, on one side the McBrides, on the other the Laveys.

16

Tonight being Friday was bath night. Mary Ann didn't mind the bath, in fact she liked it, but she hated having to provide the means for it, for no matter how she talked to herself or what games she played she found that, even with their Michael on the other side of the handle, a bucket of water weighed a ton by the time she had reached the twenty-eighth step and the top landing. If possible she would have preferred to carry the bucket herself, for their Michael was the worst one on earth for playing games. What was more, tonight being Friday her grannie was sure to be visiting. That together with the bath was enough to try an angel with nothing on her mind; Mary Ann was no angel and she had a lot on her mind.

Once upon a time, she had hated to go into the house and find her grannie there, for as sure as life her grannie would want her to go and stay with her for the week-end, and to be in her grannie's company for just one hour seemed like a long nightmare, but now, although she still hated to find her there, all fear that she would make any such disagreeable request of her was past. If she thought her grannie was going to be so foolish as to ask her to go and stay with her, she had just to look at her with a certain look, which she kept now especially for her grannie, and that terrible old lady would dry up.

For years Mrs. McMullen had put so many fears into Mary Ann's mind that it became difficult for the child to know which she was afraid of most . . . of hell, where she'd be made to sit on a red-hot gridiron all day without her knickers on, of being thrown clean out of the Catholic Church and plumb into the Salvation Army, or of being put away in a home so that she would never be able to see her ma or her da again till she would be an old woman of twenty. But now the old lady no longer instilled fear into Mary Ann with her prophecies; if possible, she kept out of her granddaughter's way, for Mary Ann had at last got her, if not exactly where she wanted her, at least under a certain control, and here she hoped to keep her. But Mary Ann knew she could only do this if she remained strong enough not to tell her da what had changed her grannie, for once she divulged the reason, her power, she knew, would vanish as quickly as a soap bubble, for he would roar for a month, and nothing she could think of would keep him from throwing his knowledge at his mother-in-law by way of a small repayment for what he had suffered at her hands during the past years.

Panting, Mary Ann reached the eighteenth stair and the landing before her own, and there, as usual, was Miss Harper, with her door open and sitting just where she could see who passed up and down.

'Hallo, there, Mary Ann,' Miss Harper called; 'your grannie's up.'

'Hallo, Miss Harper,' said Mary Ann. 'Is she?'

Unsmiling, she mounted her own flight of stairs. Miss Harper knew everybody's business, and she was the biggest borrower from here to John O' Groats.

She pushed open her own door, and there was her grannie, sitting like a lady in her astrakhan coat, and her hat, with the blue feather and veil on, cocked high upon her head.

'Hallo, Mary Ann,' said Mrs. McMullen primly.

'Hallo, Grannie,' said Mary Ann.

'Have you just come from school?'

'Yes, Grannie.' What a silly daft question. Where would she have come from? Whitley Bay?

'Get your hands washed, and you can have your tea now,' said her mother.

'Aw ... w,' Mary Ann protested, her face screwed up; 'can't I wait until me da comes?'

'Get your hands washed.'

When her mother spoke in that tone there was nothing to do but get your hands washed.

The ritual over, Mary Ann held up her hands for her mother's inspection; then sat down at the table. It was adorned with the best cloth, with the fancy work at the corners, and on a tray stood the three best cups, which if you held them up to the light you could see through, and the best tea-pot, which was of the same blue colour as the cups, but didn't match and had an odd lid.

In front of her grannie was a plate of boiled ham and a jar of pickled onions, and in the centre of the table was a plate of square, thin slices of bread which told all who beheld it that it was a 'cut loaf'.

Mary Ann watched her grannie eyeing the plate, and she said to herself, 'If she says a thing about it I'll say ... "Milk Bottles!" I will, you'll see.' And she could almost hear her grannie thinking: Bought bread again, huh! Thought she didn't hold with it ... nothing but brown, home-made wholemeal for her children. Must have their fancy vitamins. She hasn't a penny left to get the flour, that's it. And she got the loaf and ham on tick from Funnell's, I bet.

And Mary Ann also watched her mother avoid her grannie's eye and go to the fireplace. But she became so intent on again staring at her grannie that she did not notice her mother come back to the table; and she jumped when she said, 'Will you have jam or syrup?'

She eyed the small amount of jam in the dish, and knowing that Michael liked jam and hated syrup and thinking of last night and the names he had called their da, she said, 'Jam.'

'Jam what?' asked her mother.

'Please.'

'They hadn't to be told in my day,' said her grannie. Then almost choking on a mouthful of ham, she added hastily and in oiled tones to make up for her censure, 'Have you been picked for the procession, Mary Ann?'

Mary Ann attacked her jam and bread with vigour, but

made no reply; and her mother said sharply, 'You heard your grannie talking to you?'

So Mary Ann, her eyes fixed on her plate, said, 'No, Grannie.' Oh, how she hated her grannie. She always asked about things that hurt you. For two pins she'd lean across the table and look her right in her old wrinkled eyes and say, 'Milk Bottles!' But once she had said it her hold would be gone, so she contented herself with just staring at her grannie in an irritating way and thinking back to that Sunday morning and the milk bottles.

She could see herself – it was very early and she had wakened with a cramp in her stomach. She was staying in Shields with her grannie, and as she usually did on such visits she was sleeping on the couch behind the kitchen door. It was the plums that were causing the cramp. Her grannie had made her eat them because she said they shouldn't be wasted. Yet they had been all soft and nasty. She'd got up and unbolted the back door and gone out to the lavatory. She had sat there for a long time, for the cramp kept on coming and going, and during the times her stomach was at peace she thought of home and her da and whether it had been a nice week-end. If it had he would be taking some tea to her ma in bed; and if she had been at home she'd have got some too, just as if she were grown up.

It was then she saw her grannie through the crack in the door. She watched her coming stealthily down the yard; then she disappeared from her sight as she went to the back door. Puzzled, she had listened, and she had heard her grannie open the back door and close it, and when she came within sight again she was carrying two pints of milk. She saw her stand within the shelter of the staircase wall, which also kept her out of the view of the upper window; and she watched her skilfully remove the milk-caps by inserting a needle under their edges, then pour the cream off both bottles into the screw-top jar, which she took from beneath her apron. This done, she filled one of the bottles to the brim out of the other, and after carefully replacing the cap, left the bottle inside the back door.

It was at this point that Mary Ann showed herself, and she watched her grannie hang on to the door for a moment and fight for breath as she exclaimed, 'Eeh! I saw what you did.'

She thought her grannie was going to have a fit; but before she could add anything further to her accusation she was grabbed by the collar of the coat she was wearing over her nightie and lifted clean off her feet and run up the yard as if the devil had her by the neck.

But if the terrifying Mrs. McMullen had hoped to frighten Mary Ann she was mistaken. When at last Mary Ann was able to get a word in, with enraging calm and in her own words she reminded her grannie that it was only two weeks ago that Mrs. Baker from upstairs, her that was deaf, had stood in the kitchen and complained of there being no cream on the milk, and she had blamed the milkman for swiping it and feeding his large, robust family with it.

There had followed a verbal barrage for power, which ended with Mary Ann putting on her clothes and saying she thought she'd go to mass in Jarrow this morning, and if her grannie would give her the threepence now for the bus instead of the night she'd be obliged.

Mrs. McMullen had handed over the money, whilst her eyes had consigned her grandchild to the place from where through continued chastisement she had hoped to save her.

Mary Ann's last words as she left the house, which were apropos of nothing that had been said that morning, almost caused the final collapse of Mrs. McMullen, for just a second before closing the door behind her Mary Ann said, 'Me da's a grand man.'

She had often wished since she had stayed just a little longer to have seen the effect of her words on her grannie, for even through the closed door she had heard the sound of her choking.

She looked now at the old woman guzzling the last of the ham. She hadn't been offered even the smallest piece. But what did it matter? She had more than ham on her grannie, and her grannie knew it. She could keep her ham and she hoped it stuck half-way down. She looked to where her mother was refilling her grannie's cup and wondered, and not for the first time, if her grannie was really her mother's mother. Her da likely wasn't joking when he had said her grannie had stolen her mother when she was a baby and she really never had been Lizzie McMullen at all but one of the first ladies of the land. Her da joked a lot at times, but still he was probably right about this, for what connection had her lovely mother with her grannie? None; none in the wide world. Her mother's hair was fair, like silver, and straight; not even a kink in it; while her grannie's was black and white and frizzed up like a nigger's. She got it that way by sticking it in thousands of papers. And her grannie's eyes were as round as aniseed balls but black, while her mother's were long and grey. And then again her grannie was little and stumpy and fat, and her mother was a grand height, and if she'd had nice clothes like Mrs. Tullis, who kept the outdoor beershop at the corner, she'd have looked like a queen. No, like a princess; for in spite of her mother's great age of twenty-nine, she could be gay at times, like a young princess. No; her mother was no relation to her grannie. Would her mother have golloped all that ham herself? She wouldn't even eat any food if there wasn't much for her and their Michael. Her grannie was just what her da said she was, pig, guts, hog and artful!

'You can get down now.' Lizzie's voice brought Mary Ann's fixed gaze from her grandmother. 'Say your grace.'

Mary Ann said her grace. She knew why she had been

ordered to leave the table, because she'd been staring at her grannie and her ma was afraid she'd say something.

Never slow to take advantage of a situation, she asked, 'Can I look at the album, Ma?'

Now the album was a treasure chest which, through an odd assortment of snaps, kept fresh the memories of the happy incidents that had taken place in the early years of Elizabeth Shaughnessy's married life, and as time went on she found it more and more necessary to refer to it to confirm that these memories were the stamp on her mind of incidents that had once actually taken place and were not just vague dreams.

Mary Ann could remember when she first saw the album. She was sitting between her ma and da and they were laughing and laughing as they turned the pages. She could remember the firelight shining on their faces, and they had both appeared so beautiful to her that instead of laughing with them she had cried. She could remember her da picking her up and carrying her upstairs to bed. Yes, she'd gone upstairs to bed, where Michael and her had a real bedroom. She couldn't remember very much about that house, only the real bedroom. There had been other houses; then rooms; and finally Mulhattans' Hall. In each place the furniture got less and less, until now none of it was familiar ... only the album. The table and chairs might change, and even the beds, but the album ... never. It was to her a land wherein she could wander and dream; but rare were the times she was allowed to wander alone. Only on such occasions as the present when her mother desired to keep her quiet was there a chance of getting the album to herself.

She saw that her mother was annoyed with her because she had asked for the album in front of her grannie, for it was a subject of controversy between them; Mrs. McMullen considered that it belonged to her by right, having ignored the fact that her late husband had given it to his daughter on her sixteenth birthday.

'Wash your hands again,' said Lizzie; 'and be careful how you get it out of the trunk. And mind, don't disarrange the things. And stay in the room with it.'

Mary Ann did as she was bidden; and as she knelt on the floor to open the lid of the trunk that stood beside the little window which came down to the floor, she paused to wonder why the album should have been put into the trunk, for although it was usually placed out of her reach it was generally on show, for it was indeed a showpiece, being backed with fine leather and bound with brass hinges that spread across the back and front of it; it had once been owned by her mother's granda who came from Norway.

She lifted it tenderly out of the trunk, smoothed again into order the assortment of clothes, then went to the bed and, laying it there, she fell on her stomach across the bed, her heels playing a silent tattoo on her small buttocks. Sucking in her breath in anticipation of coming enjoyment, she lifted back the heavy cover and looked once more on Great-Granda Stenson. But his sidewhiskers had long ceased to be funny. She turned a number of thick pages, ignoring with an upward tilt of her nose the photographs they held; she knew them all; they were merely pictures of her grannie from the time she was a baby until she was married ... and who'd want to look at them? But following the picture of her grandmother's wedding group the real pictures began.

Now she burrowed her knees into the bed. There was her ma with nothing on; and there was her ma on the sands with her spade and pail; and there she was again with her great long fair plaits and holding her school prize in her hand. There were many more snaps of her ma. Then they too abruptly stopped, and Mary Ann was confronted with two blank pages. They were like a curtain ending an act of a play, and although she was anxious to raise the curtain and

24

continue the story, she did not hurry, but savoured what was to come. She knew there was not a lot more to follow, but it was the best, and, like the pork cracknel she sometimes had on a Sunday, she always conserved the nice things until the end.

Slowly now she turned the page, and there they were, her ma and da. She drew the air up through her nose as if inhaling a scent. Oh, didn't they look lovely? Anybody would know that her ma was a bride although she wasn't dressed in white but just in a costume. It was the . . . lovely look on her face that told you. And there was her da, dressed as a soldier. Oh, better than a soldier . . . an airman. And he wasn't just like any airman, for he had two stripes on his arm. He'd been a grand man in the Air Force, had her da. He had told her about the marshal, the one that sent the aeroplanes up. He had thought the world of her da, and he wouldn't think about lifting a finger unless first asking her da about it. . . . Oh my, yes; it was as her da said, the Air Force knew it the day he left.

Her ma, at one time, had laughed until she cried when her da was telling her about what a grand man he was in the Air Force. But not lately, not since they came to live here. In fact, when she came to think about it, her da never looked at the album at all now.

Suddenly her interest in the pictures waned; she found she didn't want to look at herself and their Michael in the various stages of undress. She looked up from the book and around the room. Its only articles of furniture were the bed, the trunk and a white-painted wardrobe. The floor had no covering except a clippie rug, but the boards were stained and polished and would have looked fine, she thought, had there not been so many wide gaps that let both draught and dust up through them.

Slowly she closed the book and wriggled back off the bed; and lifting the album, she returned it to the trunk. And not until she had closed the lid did she realize that it was the very first time she had put it away without being told ... always her mother had to tell her again and again before she could be induced to close it. A pain not unlike a toothache came into her chest, and she stepped to the window and stood looking down into the street. Some of her friends were playing tiggie in the middle of the road, while others on the pavement opposite were endeavouring to walk on tin cans which they held tight to the soles of their shoes by pulling on string reins. The hurt feeling was pressing on her so heavily that it took away the wish that she might join them.

Her mind became a confused jumble of desires. They swirled around in her head and became tangled, as always, about the mainspring of her life; if only her ma and da laughed together like they used to; if only their Michael didn't make her wild by saying the things he did about her da; if only there were no week-ends in the week and men didn't get paid on a Friday; and if only her grannie could be wafted away to some far place; not hell; no, but some place from where she would find it impossible to come and visit her ma and talk in a quiet voice in the scullery, telling her what she should do about her da – her ma was always short with him after her grannie had been.

She leaned her head against the top of the attic window – it was just the right height for leaning against – and filled now with a pain that was almost of an adult quality, she stared unseeing through it.

Usually she was only too well aware that the Flannagans' window was straight below theirs on the opposite side of the street; but this evening with so much on her mind she gave no thought to it, until the curtains being jerked violently together attracted her attention. Then she straightened herself up, thinking, Eeh, I wasn't looking in. Eeh, I wasn't. She was about to withdraw when a too-well-known face suddenly appeared between the curtains and a tongue of remarkable length was thrust up at her. Before she could retaliate the owner of the tongue had withdrawn it, and the curtains were again closed.

For the moment, the weight of the family worry was lifted from her, and she compressed her lips and shook her head from side to side before muttering, 'Oh, Sarah Flannagan, you cheeky thing, you. Oh, you are! Just you wait.'

She could see by the bunched curtains that her enemy was still behind them, so keeping to one side of the attic window she waited, and it was no time at all before the curtains were jerked apart, and Mary Ann was ready at the instant. Not only did her tongue shoot out but it wagged itself violently for a second before returning limply to its residence.

Gasping with indignation, Mrs. Flannagan threw up the window; but Mary Ann did not wait to hear what she had to say. With her fingers pressed to her lips she ran across the room, but before pulling open the door she composed herself to enter the kitchen so as not to give herself away. But she need not have troubled, for her mother and her grannie were in the scullery, as her grannie's voice proclaimed.

It came softly, but clearly audible, to her. 'You're a fool,' it said.

She stood, her ear cocked towards the scullery, and when her grannie's voice came again, her body began to tremble as if she was freezing with cold. 'Leave him. Get a court order; he'll have to pay. I'll take the bairns. And if you don't want to go back to office work there's plenty of clean factories to pick from now. If ever there's been a fool, it's you. If only you'd stuck to Bob Quinton you'd be living like a lady now. Look at the building business he's got up. And him never married. Oh, I wish the other one would fall into the Don on a dark night, I do, so help me God. And there's never a night goes by but I pray for it. God forgive me.'

There was a crash that brought the two women running into the kitchen, and for a moment they stood looking down at the blue cup and saucer lying in fragments on the hearth. Then they looked towards Mary Ann standing by the table, her face white and drained and her eyes stretched wide.

Mrs. McMullen was the first to speak. Forgetting for the moment all caution, she reverted to her old manner. 'Well now, would you believe it? Anybody can see with half an eye that she threw it. Well, I ask you. And one of the good ones, an' all.'

'Shut up! Shut up! Shut up!' The words rose to a scream in Mary Ann's throat. The tears rained from her eyes, blinding her. As her mother's arms went about her she started to moan, and Lizzie, holding her tightly, cried, 'It's all right. It's all right. It doesn't matter about the cup or anything. We'll get another. Sh! . . . Sh! now.'

'A good smacked backside, that's what she wants.'

'Mother. Please.' Lizzie's voice checked the old woman. 'Go, will you; I'll be down on Sunday.'

Even the feather on Mrs. McMullen's hat seemed to bristle. 'You're telling me to get out because of that 'un?'

'Yes. Yes. Don't you see? Just this once. Go on.'

Completely outraged, Mrs. McMullen buttoned up her coat and marched to the door. But there she turned and said, 'Very well. But I'll expect you as usual on Sunday, mind. What's things coming to, anyway? Ordered out!' Her voice was cut off abruptly from them as the door banged.

For a moment Lizzie's eyes rested on the closed door; then lifting Mary Ann up she set her on her knee and rocked her gently, saying nothing but looking away out of the window, over the roof tops, into a narrow stretch of clear sky, unpierced by even one tall chimney or crane or mast.

Was it wrong to wish to die? Was it wrong to wish from the bottom of her heart that she had never set eyes on Mike Shaughnessy? How much longer could she go on? . . . All her life, she supposed, until she was an old woman, inured to it

28

all like Mrs. Lavey down below ... hope dead, love and respect burnt out. What more could she do? Only pray for something to happen. She shook her head. Pray? She was always praying, until now it had become only a form of talking to herself. Sometimes she thought her appeals never left her head – there was no force left in her to push them out. Her belief in the goodness of God was going, if not already gone. To believe in God's inevitable pattern for good you had to be made like Mary Ann and swear black was white, or be a saint. She was long past the Mary Ann stage, and she wasn't made of the stuff of saints. She wanted to lead a decent life and to have Mike the way he used to be. She wouldn't grow into a Mrs. Lavey; she'd leave him.

She almost sprang to her feet, forgetting that she held the child.

The jerk caused Mary Ann to slip to the floor, and she stood dazed, and asked, 'Is he coming? Is it me da?'

'No,' said Lizzie, getting up; 'you slipped.'

'Ma.'

'Yes?'

'Me grannie ...'

'Now' – Lizzie smoothed the tumbled hair back from Mary Ann's forehead – 'forget what you heard your grannie say.'

'But she said ...'

'It doesn't matter what she said. Everything's going to be all right.'

'Honest?'

Lizzie pressed her teeth into her lip and her head moved slightly. 'Honest,' she said.

Mary Ann sniffed and turned away. 'Will I start getting the water up?'

'No. Wait until Michael comes in,' said Lizzie.

'But he won't be in until six. Didn't he say that Mr. Wilson wanted him for two hours the night?'

'Yes, I know. But it can wait until he comes in. You can go out and play for a little while.'

'I don't want to go.'

Lizzie looked down on her daughter, and she thought, Oh, let her want to go out to play. Don't let her start to reason and feel yet. But hadn't she always reasoned and felt, especially where he was concerned? If things came to a pitch, it would be her that would be the stumbling-block. If she were deprived of him she would die. She said, 'Do you want the album again?'

'No.' Mary Ann shook her head. And as Lizzie stared at her the sound of footsteps on the stairs caused them both to turn and face the door, but almost instantly they recognized the steps weren't his.

There came a knock on the door, and when Lizzie opened it there stood Mrs. Flannagan dressed for the street; and besides wearing her best things she was using her best voice, the one that Mike Shaughnessy called her refeened twang.

'Mrs. Shaughnessy, I must have a word with you. I'm sorry to trouble you as you've plenty on your plate, God knows, but I really must make a stand. It's getting that way that a body can't look out of her window.'

'What has she done now?' Lizzie Shaughnessy's voice was flat.

'Stuck her tongue out at me. A yard long it was. I was just pulling back me curtains before I went out. I was just off to the confraternity . . . I'll let the sun in, I thought, to warm up the room. It's a pity you don't get it across this way in the evening, it'd make all the difference. But there I was at the window, and she came and with real intent and purpose she leant forward and stuck her tongue out at me. I was so taken aback, Mrs. Shaughnessy, I was really. It was uncalled for.'

'Did you?' Lizzie looked over her shoulder to where Mary Ann was standing behind her.

'Not at her, Ma. At Sarah. She had stuck her tongue out at me and dived behind the curtains; and I was waiting for her.'

'Now, now, now, Mary Ann.' Mrs. Flannagan looked and sounded distinctly shocked. 'My Sarah was nowhere in the room, when I went to the window. You must not pree-varitate.'

'I'm not,' said Mary Ann from behind her mother. 'She was. I saw her through the curtains.'

'Well! ... That child!' To Mrs. Flannagan's feelings was added indignation. 'It's one thing to weave tales as I know you do, but it's another thing to tell downright lies. I'll say no more, Mrs. Shaughnessy. But I thought I'd come and tell you ... one must make a stand. And I'm not a person to cause trouble, especially to those who are heavily burdened already.'

Mary Ann saw her mother's shoulders lift and heard her voice take on that note that made her different. 'You came to tell me about Mary Ann putting her tongue out. You have told me, Mrs. Flannagan. I shall chastise Mary Ann. Is there anything more you want to say to me?'

There followed a short silence while the two women regarded each other. Then the older woman burst out, 'Don't come your hoity-toity with me, Mrs. Shaughnessy; it won't wash. I pity you, I do, but I'll only stand so much.'

'Your pity is entirely wasted, Mrs. Flannagan. ...'

'It is that. It is that.' The deep rocketing voice came from the stairs, and Mary Ann sprang forward, only to be stopped by her mother's hip. She watched her father come into view, but he didn't look to where she was or at her mother, but straight at Mrs. Flannagan.

'Good evening to you, Mrs. Flannagan.' He doffed his black, grease-laden cap, and standing over the now wide-eyed Mrs. Flannagan, he held it to his chest and moved it round between his hands in mock obsequiousness, and his voice took on a matching whine. 'Your pity's wasted on me wife, Mrs. Flannagan. But now me, it's the very thing I'm needing. I'm needing pity so badly that you could bath me in it; you could hold me down in a bath full of it and I wouldn't drown. It has the same effect on me as beer, you know. Now, now, what's your hurry?' he obstructed her means of escape by standing at the head of the stairs. 'Don't go away, Mrs. Flannagan, without sprinkling on me shamed head a few drops of your pity. It'd be about as effective as your holy water.'

'Mike!'

Mike took not the slightest notice of his wife's sharp demand, but advanced one step further towards the now retreating woman saying, 'Come now. Come now. You must make a stand. That's it, isn't it? That's your slogan ... you must make a stand.'

'I'll call me husband, mind.'

Mike Shaughnessy's head went back and he bellowed forth a laugh. 'You've got a sense of humour, I'll grant you that.' Then of a sudden he dropped his posing and his voice lost its bantering tone, and he stood to one side, and, pointing to the stairs, said, 'Get down there, and don't come up here again unless you're asked, for if I find you at this door again I'll put me toe in your backside. That's if I'm sober. God knows what I'll do to you if I'm drunk.' He watched her scurrying down the stairs; then he turned to his own doorway, which was now empty, and entered the room.

Lizzie was at the table and did not look towards him, nor he to her, but he threw his cap to Mary Ann and she caught it deftly. Then she took his greasy mackintosh and dived into the inner pocket where his bait tin was, and opening it, discovered there one sausage. She smiled at him, and taking it out sniffed its smoky, stale flavour, then began to eat it hurriedly before her ma should remember it was Friday and stop her.

Mike divested himself of his coat, and, rolling up his sleeves, went towards the scullery, saying, 'What brought her here?'

Mary Ann and Lizzie exchanged glances. Then Mary Ann said, 'I put me tongue out at her; I thought she was Sarah behind the curtains.'

His head went up again, and he laughed 'Good for you.'

Mary Ann lifted the kettle from the hob and followed him into the scullery. She poured the water into a dish and stood waiting at his side with the towel while he washed himself. He did this with a lot of puffing and blowing, interspersed with remarks about Mrs. Flannagan.

'You know the saying: "Put a beggar on horseback and he'll ride to Hell?" Well, it was started by just such another as her. Did you know that?'

'No, Da.'

'Well, it was. She means to rise, that 'un, or die in the attempt. It's a good job the poor are kept down.' He blew into the towel. Then peering over the top of it his brown eyes twinkled down at her. 'You remember the time she sent the note to your school saying Sarah had an illustrated throat?'

Mary Ann laughed up at him. She remembered it well. The note had been passed among the teachers and they had not been discreet about the cause of their laughter.

'And there was the time she asked in Funnell's for the liquidated milk. Do you mind that?'

Mary Ann nodded and chuckled, saying, 'If she couldn't have said evaporated she should have said unsweetened, shouldn't she?'

'She should that.' He buttoned up his shirt neck. 'Take my tip, Mary Ann. Anyone who tries to use long words in an aim to get above themselves, they're not much good. You can say all you want to say with your own kind of language.'

'But if you could get to the Grammar School you'd learn big words then properly, wouldn't you?'

'Yes . . . yes, you would then.'

'If Michael goes, he'll learn big words.'

Mike stopped in the act of rolling down his shirt sleeves and stared at her; but she did not flinch from the look in his eyes.

She might fight with Michael because he called this man names – Michael sometimes lay on the floor and beat his fists on the mat, grinding out from between his teeth such words as 'Big, rotten, drunken beast!' At such times she hated Michael and would think nothing of kicking out at him. Yet she knew why Michael said these things. He loved their mother and he was hurt when she was hurt, and he was ashamed of their da. He was going in for an exam for the Grammar School and he couldn't see himself holding a place there when his father's name was becoming a byword wherever drunks were mentioned – but her eyes were now telling Mike Shaughnessy that no matter how she fought with Michael she wanted him to go to the Grammar School, not so as she could brag about him, but because it would make her ma happy.

Suddenly Mike took her small face between his great hands and pressed it gently, and she pressed her hands over his before turning swiftly and running into the kitchen.

'Where's the kettle?' asked her mother.

'Oh!' She turned about again and collided with her father, and they both laughed.

Mike went to the table and looked significantly down on to the empty plates set there, and Lizzie, still not looking at him said, 'I didn't get anything ready.'

Mike gazed at his wife in silence for a moment before saying, 'You didn't believe me then?'

Lizzie moved towards the fire, and his eyes followed her.

'I swore to you.'

'You've sworn before.'

'But I thought it was a fresh start?'

Lizzie stood looking down into the fire, and he came and stood behind her, his red head topping her silver one. 'Liz' – his arms went about her – 'help me; I am trying hard.'

She did not answer but made a choking sound, and he swung her round to him and held her pressed tightly against his chest.

Mary Ann stood at the door of the scullery, her eyes bright, watching them. It caused her no embarrassment to see her parents loving; rather, it filled her with bubbling joy. She listened now to her da's voice deep in his throat, and soft.

'Darlin', darlin'. I swear before God I'll make a go of it this time. Liz, Oh Liz. I should be hung for the things I've done to you.' His voice became lower. 'Never leave me, Liz. Promise you'll never leave me.'

No answer came from her mother, only the sound of her sobs. They were too much for Mary Ann and she turned into the scullery and, leaning against the wall, began to cry. Oh it was going to be a lovely week-end. Oh her da was wonderful.

There was no connection between the man in there saying such words as darlin', beloved and precious, and the man who, just a week tonight, had rolled up the stairs at eleven o'clock singing at the top of his voice and proclaiming to all who would listen to him that at this time tomorrow he'd be a rich man, for hadn't he put three pounds on a sure winner, and the Sporting Pink would be red with his success.

There was no sound now from the kitchen, and after drying her eyes Mary Ann went in. Her mother was standing by the table opening her da's pay packet. She watched her shake out the contents. It was all happening as she had heard him saying last night it would.

Lizzie counted the notes, then moved the silver about with her finger. There was thirteen shillings, and she looked up at her husband and said, 'Will that do?'

He stared at it for a moment; then smiled with the corner of his mouth drawn in. 'Make it a quid. That'll do for me baccy an' all.'

She handed him the pound, and taking another four from the bundle of seven she stuck them in a jug on the mantelpiece, saying, 'That'll clear the rent.'

'Ah, Liz-a-beth. Must you do it all at once?'

His tone was joking, but Mary Ann knew that he didn't like what her ma had done.

'Look' – he caught hold of Lizzie's arm – 'pay two weeks. You can clear it next week. You'll have more next week. I'm telling you, you will. What do you think? Look at me now' – he drew himself up a mock attitude – 'and listen to what I am saying. Mike Shaughnessy is working the morrer – overtime till five.'

Lizzie and Mary Ann stared at him but said nothing, and he dived across the kitchen and, lifting a chair, brought it to Lizzie, saying, 'Hold on to that, for you'll need it.' He put her hands on the back of it, then stood away from her and proclaimed in an awful voice, 'Sunday an' all!'

Now Lizzie did show her surprise, and her expression gave him great delight; and Mary Ann stared up at her father her eyes like pools of gladness. He was going to do overtime; he was going to work on a Sunday; he must have forgotten clean about the things he called theories, for they usually stopped him doing overtime. He often had these theories when he was having a period of ... sickness, and then he would talk a lot about them. She had come to understand that if all the men did overtime there soon wouldn't be enough work for them in the middle of the week, and they would be standing at the street corners again. She couldn't imagine the men standing at the street corners in the middle of the week, except Willie James, and he'd neither work nor want. Sometimes her da's theories took a different turn, as they had done last week-end when he talked all the time about the men stopping work on account of Harry Bancroft being sacked. He said Harry Bancroft had asked for it for he'd never done a decent day's work in his life; then he got bitter and said nobody had wanted to strike when he'd got the push, yet he did more work in a day than some of them did in a week, for he wasn't a gaffer watcher; and if every man pulled his weight there'd be no need for overtime. And he knew why he had got the sack. It was because he'd made his mouth go against the Union.

And now he was going to do overtime, and they'd have a lot of money next week and her ma would be happy and not listen to her grannie.

She ran to him, and throwing her arms round his leg clutched it to her. Mike laid his hand upon his daughter's head, and still looking at his wife, said, 'See? You see? I have me public.' Then hoisting Mary Ann into his arms, he kissed her and asked, 'Do you know what your da's going to do the morrer night?' And she, holding his beloved face gently between her hands as if it were something delicate and precious, said, 'Take us into Shields.'

He sniffed loudly. 'Shields! Newcastle it is the morrer night, and we're going to do a show; and in style.'

'Don't buoy her up.' Lizzie spoke quietly. 'I'm paying all the rent and you'll want your pound for baccy and for fares. And there's a bill to pay to Funnell's.'

'But I tell you I'll make a fiver over the week-end – you can pay it off next week.' He put Mary Ann down and moved towards his wife, saying, 'Ah Liz, be reasonable.'

But Lizzie moved away from him and went to the mantelpiece, and, taking the four pounds out of the jug, she turned to Mary Ann saying, 'Straighten your hair and put your hat and coat on.'

'What you going to do?' Mike's voice was stiff now.

'Send it to him.' Lizzie sat down at the table, and having written a note, put it with the money in an envelope, and when Mary Ann stood by her side, she said, 'Now you know where to go, don't you? Along Grange Road and turn to the right.'

'I know,' said Mary Ann. Her voice, too, was flat and had a touch of impatience in it. Oh, if only her ma hadn't got to do it. But she had; and there was her da looking at them, his face all hard again.

Her mother pinned the envelope inside the breast pocket of her school frock. 'Go on now, and don't speak to anyone; and keep to the main roads.'

As she moved towards the door no one spoke, and when she went out, closing the door after her, and stood on the landing, still no sound came from the room to her. An urgent, turbulent feeling filled her stomach. It had a voice of its own which cried loudly in her ears, 'Make them speak. Oh, make them speak. It'll soon be all right if they'll only speak.' She waited, her head bent towards the door; she couldn't go all the way down Western Road and Ormond Street across Dee Street to Grange Road to the rent man's house knowing they were not speaking.

'You're not taking any chances on me, are you?'

In spite of her relief, the tone of her father's voice hurt her; and her mother's added to the pain as she said, 'I've been taken in before; you wouldn't have rested until you'd had that rent.'

'My God! After all I said last night. All I was asking was that you paid two weeks and cleared it next. I wanted to give you a treat ... take you away out of here for a while.'

'I'd rather get out of here permanently.'

'You shall, Liz – you shall, but I can't do it all at once.'

Her father's voice was so convincing; how could anyone

not believe him. And it went on, 'Do you know it's Hell now – this minute my innards are burning for a drink.'

'Mike. Oh, Mike!'

There was a scrambling sound, and she knew her mother had flown to her da and that her arms were about him and that she was soothing and mothering him like she did Michael and herself when they were bad. Filled now with a sad happiness, she was about to turn from the door when a voice hissing between the banisters caused her to jump.

'You sneaking little pig. Just you wait – I'll tell me ma. Listening at the key-hole again.'

'Aw! you,' she hissed back at her brother. 'I wasn't listening.'

When Michael reached the landing he towered above her, his indignation making him seem even taller. In looks at least he took after his father; and he already looked more than his eleven years, whereas Mary Ann looked less than her eight; but in repartee and temper they were equally matched.

'I'd like to box your ears.'

'I know.' She pursed up her lips and wagged her head at him. 'But you'll have to grow a bit more, Michael Shaughnessy; and if you raise a hand to me I'll bite a lump out of you – see?' She edged round him and made her way down a number of stairs before turning and looking up into his angry countenance, and calling softly, 'Ginger! you're barmy.'

She did not stop to find out whether or not he was after her but took the stairs at a dangerous speed, almost taking Miss Harper's dustbin with her. But once she had gained the hall and found that she wasn't being pursued, her bearing suddenly changed and took on a graveness, as befitted anyone with a fortune pinned on her chest.

CHAPTER THREE

SATURDAY

It was a funny Saturday, Mary Ann reflected, her da being at work in the afternoon; and it was pouring from the heavens and she couldn't go out; and it was cold, too. She was sitting on the fender near the oven where she was both warm and lapped around with the appetizing aroma of baking. The bread was out and arranged on the rack above her head, and inside the oven a bacon and egg pie was cooking. Her da liked bacon and egg pie. And her mother looked happier today and nearly young again – twice she had laughed at her when she'd had to push her along the fender to get to the oven.

Michael was sitting at the corner of the table writing on scraps of paper. He was doing sums. He hadn't passed the exam last year, and she wasn't a bit surprised, getting sums like he had to do. His teacher said he should have passed on his head. The teacher had come and talked to her ma and said Michael was worried and highly-strung and nervous. She was glad she wasn't going in for any exam. She didn't hate Michael today, she was sorry for him, yet last night she had stamped hard on his bare foot and pretended it was an accident. She had done that because he wouldn't answer their da nicely when he talked to him. Her da wasn't sick, even a little bit, because he had never been out, and he had asked Michael about the exam, and Michael had been surly and said, 'Oh, what's the use?' And he had gone out of the room and she had followed him and stamped on his bare toe. But today he too seemed happier, and he had been working at his sums all afternoon, except when he talked to their ma. Sometimes he talked quietly so that she wouldn't hear. She wasn't in the least annoyed at this because she liked to talk to her da in that way. Michael was talking quietly now, and she was pretending to read her comic while straining her ears to hear what he was saying. He was talking about clothes.

'I'd need a sweater and sports things; it wouldn't matter about a top coat, I never feel the cold.'

'Don't worry about anything.' His mother's voice was as low as his. 'You'll get all the things you need; you must keep all you earn from now on to help buy what's necessary.'

'Oh, no.'

'Yes.'

'Well, I will just this week.'

Why, Mary Ann wondered, should he want to keep his money just this week? And then with a start she remembered April the twenty-third was her mother's birthday, and today. ... What was today? Yesterday at school had been the fifteenth; then this was the sixteenth. A week today! And she had nothing saved up. Well, only three-pence. Still, she had to get her pay from her da yet. But that would only be sixpence at the most. She looked towards her mother's back. The skirt and jumper she was wearing both had a washed-out look. Oh, if only she had a lot of money and could go and buy her a dress. If she had a pound she'd buy her a lovely dress. There was a shop down Ormond Street that had lovely dresses. She had touched one once. There was a rack just inside the door and she had seen a woman pushing the dresses back and forward, and she had slipped in and stood behind the rack and fingered the dresses until the shop-woman had found her and chased her. Now, if she could buy her mother one of those dresses. If she could make a lot of money ... oh, if only she knew the way to

41

make some money. She was no good at knitting and selling things, or making kettle holders. Perhaps if she asked the Holy Family they'd show her the way. Yes, that was it. Bowing her head farther over her comic and pretending to read, she began supplicating conversation with the Holy Family.

'Are you in, Lizzie?' A voice broke in on her prayers, and exclaiming, 'Oh bust!' she raised her head.

It was Mrs. McBride. Not that she disliked Mrs. McBride, but she talked a lot and everything had been so nice, just the three of them; and now their Michael would go into the other room to do his work and it was cold in there.

'Come in, Mrs. McBride.' Her mother never called Mrs. McBride Fanny, like the other women in the house.

'Oh, these stairs, I don't know how you stand them.'

'Sit down. Get Mrs. McBride a chair, Michael.'

Michael brought a chair forward and placed it near the fat old woman, then without a word he gathered up his papers from the table and went out of the room.

'Thanks, lad,' Fanny called after him. 'He still working at his books?' She looked up at Lizzie, and without waiting for any comment she went on, 'What I came up about was Lady Golightly. I've just heard this minute that she was over here last night and that Mike put a flea in her ear. Oh, I wish I'd been in; I'd have had a reception committee on the ground floor for her, fit for the Mechanics Institute. What was she after, Lizzie?'

'Oh' – Lizzie measured the jam into the tarts – 'Mary Ann and Sarah had been having a squabble.'

'And what did Mike say to her?' Fanny asked, leaning across the table, eagerness expressed in each wrinkle of her sagging cheeks.

Lizzie laughed tolerantly and shook her head. 'I can't remember.'

Fanny sat back and with a sidelong glance looked up at

Lizzie. She scratched herself under the breasts, then rubbed the end of her nose before asking 'Is it true what I'm hearing the day?'

With a touch of asperity Lizzie replied, 'Yes, it's true.'

'Well, well.' Fanny's face was beaming. 'He'll be workin' on a Sunday next.'

'He is.'

'Glory be to God! The things you live to see.' This indeed had the power to startle Mrs. McBride and she shook her head. Then pointing a grimy finger at Lizzie, she cried, 'But you'll stand by me when I say I've always upheld Mike. Now, haven't I? Haven't I said time and again he's got one fault, and apart from that there's not a better fellow living?'

Mary Ann raised her eyes from the comic. Oh, she liked Mrs. McBride. Oh, she did.

'And he's got eyes for no one but yourself – that's another thing in his favour – drunk or sober.'

'Sh!' Lizzie's voice came sharply.

'Oh, she's reading,' said Fanny, waving Mary Ann's presence away with her hand; and she went on, 'And I'm telling you, in a way you're lucky, for some of the flaming Janes round here would put up with his weakness just to have him around the house, for where will you see a better set-up man when he's sober? Or drunk, for that matter? I've known him for longer than anybody – I should know.'

'Sh! sh!'

Fanny sighed in exasperation. 'Why bother what they hear? You cannot keep them in glasshouses, they'll go their own road, some up, some down. Oh' – she leant back and began to laugh – 'that reminds me. You'll never guess who our Phil's taken up with. Oh my, talk about reforming. What a week we've had! He's started courting a lass from Binns' – Binns' mind.' Her watery blue eyes narrowed. 'Stick that in your gullet and try to swallow. From no potty little draper's shop, but Binns' in King Street, in Shields!'

'Well, why shouldn't he? Phil's a nice lad.'

'Ay, he's nice enough; but we aren't.' Again she leaned back and laughed. 'Oh, my God!' – she slapped her thick thigh – 'you should have heard him last night at our Peggy's young Joe. "You shouldn't say backside," he said, "you should say bottom." He had cornered him in the scullery. And there was me – I had to sit down on the fender or I'd have collapsed. Joe's backside was no longer a backside but a bottom, and all because of a lass from Binns'.'

Lizzie, trying hard not to laugh, said, 'I shouldn't tease him – he wants to get on and he likely wants the girl – you should help him.'

'Help him!' Fanny's voice rose in a crescendo. 'Me help our Phil? Why Lizzie, nobody can help our Phil. It's him that's out to reform the world. You know he's never been one of us, has Phil; you could never tell where you had him or what he was up to; not like our Jack. Now he's as clear as daylight, is Jack.' She sat back, quiet for a time, savouring the affinity between herself and her youngest son. Then suddenly leaning forward again, she said, 'Did you hear about Lady Jane Collins and the rent man?'

'Mary Ann!' Lizzie turned sharply. 'Go in and play with Michael.'

'But he's doing his homework, Ma.'

'Here,' Fanny beckoned Mary Ann to her, 'go down to our house, there's nobody in, and in the pantry behind the basin of dripping on the top shelf you'll find a bar of taffy. Take half of it. Go on now.'

'Can I?' Mary Ann looked at her mother, and Lizzie nodded. Mary Ann knew why she was being allowed to go in to Mrs. McBride's. Her ma was afraid she'd hear something, like the time Mrs. McBride had talked of how she had first seen her da as a little baby in the workhouse nursery. Mary Ann didn't want to recall this, although it didn't hurt now

44

like it used to, not since her ma had made it into a story.

She did not immediately go down to Mrs. McBride's but sat on the top stair thinking of and loving and pitying her da for not having had a ma and a da and for having been brought up in a Cottage Home.

She had first heard about this when Mrs. McBride had laughed at her da for talking stronger Irish when he was sick. Mrs. McBride had stood in their kitchen and said, 'Ah, Mike, it's real funny to hear you, and you never having set foot in the country. You talk it better than either me or me Colin ever did. God have mercy on him wherever He's put him.'

Mrs. McBride had said a lot more, and her da had laughed, but it wasn't his nice laugh and her ma had pushed her outside and she had sat just here and cried. She had cried at intervals for a long time after that and then her ma had told her the story. And it went like this. Once upon a time an angel laid a baby in a basket outside Harton Institution gates. ... No, no, she wouldn't think about it. She shuffled her bottom along the bare stair board to the wall. She'd begin where her da was a grand looking lad and worked on a farm, and her ma used to cycle past and watch him work the plough. ... No, for that was a sad part too, for her grannie had found out and evacuated her ma miles and miles away. No; she'd begin where her ma was going along the platform on Hereford Station and she turned and looked towards the barrier, and there waving wildly was a man in R.A.F. uniform, and he was waving to her, and it was the boy with the red hair. She had walked back and through the barrier to his side, and when she stood near him he hadn't the sense to open his mouth.

Mary Ann sighed. That was the nice part of the story. It wasn't her ma, though, who told her how her grannie had tried to stop them getting married, it was her da, one day when he was – sick. Nor did her ma tell her that when her da

45

came out of the Air Force he went to work on a farm near Kibblesworth, but that he wouldn't stay because he couldn't get a place where they could all live together; and he had come into the town and had worked for a time in Lord's yard before getting another job on a farm. But again he couldn't get a cottage, so once more he had come back to where they were then living in a house that had its own back-yard, and even a three foot wide piece of garden in front with an iron rail round it. Yet even in all this space he said he couldn't breathe – there was no air in his lungs. It was in that house she first remembered seeing him sick. Her ma never spoke of these things, but her grannie did.

Slowly now she went down stairs, past Miss Harper's open door, down the next flight and to the hall-way, and as there was no one in she did not trouble to knock on the McBride's door but pushed it open and walked across the room that was cluttered with furniture, all very much the worse for wear. But before reaching the scullery door she stopped and her head went to one side as it was wont to do when she was surprised or interested, and added to this her eyes now opened wide and her lips slowly parted, for her astonished gaze was resting on a couple locked tightly in each other's arms. Although their faces were so close together as to be one, she knew the man to be Jack McBride and the girl, Joyce Scallen.

Now she was not unused to seeing courting couples. When she came from confession on a Thursday night and it was dark she often bumped into them at the corner of the back lane, and their bemused swaying only evoked the term 'Sloppy doppies!' from her. But this couple was different. This girl was Joyce Scallen and she was a Protestant. Worse than a Protestant – her da was in the Salvation Army, and everybody knew that Protestants, especially Salvationists, were destined for Hell. This had always made Mary Ann feel sorry, at least for Joyce, for she was so nice, and up to

46

now she had steadfastly refused to believe that every one of the Protestants would go to Hell, for this would include her da. Yet somewhere in her was the knowledge that once the Holy Family had had time to answer her special prayer on that subject and her da ... turned, then there would be no further anxiety about the destination of the Protestant tribe, singly or collectively. But eeh! for Joyce Scallen to be kissing Jack McBride – and in the McBride's scullery an' all.

The joined figures parted and Joyce's voice came pleadingly, 'Oh Jack, let me go. You shouldn't have pulled me in; there'll be murder if I'm caught.'

'It's all right, she's upstairs; she won't be down for a while and you can hear her coming a mile off.'

'But I must go; me ma'll be in shortly and someone may come.'

'Will you see me the night?'

'I can't get out – there's a meeting.'

'Then tomorrow?'

'Oh – I don't know.'

'Look, we can't go on like this. Anyway, everybody knows about us but your folks and mine, and they're laughing, waiting for the balloon to go up.'

'Yes, and when it goes up think of me da. And just imagine how your ma'll go on.'

Yes, Mary Ann thought, Mr. Scallen would create, but what would Mrs. McBride do? Eeh! she couldn't make her mind imagine the scene that would ensue when Mrs. McBride got to know.

At this point her quick ears heard a familiar voice – it was Don McBride talking to his wife as they came up the steps of the house. In a matter of seconds they'd be in the room and Jack and Joyce would be caught. Wildly, she looked about her as if she herself were trapped; then she decided there was only one thing for it. Swiftly, she dived into the scullery and her sudden appearance brought a scream from Joyce. But standing with her back to the door, she did a wild pantomime that could not have been misunderstood by the dimmest. Joyce needed no other warning. Like lightning she darted out of the back door, down the yard and into her own door opposite, while Jack stood looking down at Mary Ann, who was now beginning to enjoy herself and feeling completely in command of any wits that were left to the short thick-set young man.

'Taffy,' she whispered. 'Bunk me up to the top shelf.' The need for caution was gone but she wished to continue her part as long as possible.

As the voice of his brother came from the room Jack hoisted Mary Ann up to the shelf and hissed as he did so, 'How long have you been here?'

On the ground once more and calmly breaking the bar of toffee in two Mary Ann said, 'Oh a long time – I'll go out this way.'

'Did you see—?'

She nodded, looking straight up at him.

She had reached the door when he thrust his hand into his pocket and brought forth a handful of silver. He raked amongst it and taking out half-a-crown pushed it into her hand, saying, 'You won't let on to me ma?'

Mary Ann looked down at this gift from Heaven and murmured, 'Thank you, oh thank you, Jack.'

She was half out of the door when she turned back and whispered, 'But I wouldn't have let on anyway, you know.'

Suddenly they smiled at each other and she darted away out of the yard, round the corner and up the front steps again, and not until she had reached the comparative privacy of her own landing did she open her closed fist to make sure her eyes had not deceived her. Half-a-crown! And just for doing that. She had only to help another seven courting couples and she'd have a pound! She looked up at the

stained and peeling sloping ceiling of the staircase. . . . Oh
Jesus, Mary and Joseph, thank you very much for showing
me the way. . . . Now who would have believed they would
have been as quick as that? She had only asked them a few
minutes since. She shook her head at the tangible power of
the Holy Family.

* * *

At half past five the table was set ready and Mary Ann,
surveying it, thought that she had never seen a better. There
was a knife and fork laid for her da, which meant he was
going to have a dinner; then there was the bacon and egg
pie, and besides that jam tarts and tea-cakes, and a big sly
cake. She moved around the table examining it from all
angles. Her mouth was watering and she was hungry, but she
resisted the desire to ask for even a piece of bread because she
wanted to eat a big tea; her da liked to see her eat well.

She looked at the clock. Only another five minutes and
he'd be in. She looked at her mother. Lizzie was sitting by the
fire patching, and occasionally she too would look up at the
mantelpiece and glance at the clock. She hadn't spoken for a
long time now.

Mary Ann went and sat on the fender near Michael. For
once he wasn't writing, but just sitting gazing into the fire.
The three of them were all tidied up as if it was an occasion.
These last five minutes, she decided, were going to be the
longest in the afternoon.

She nudged Michael and asked, 'Can I have a look at your
Eagle?'

'I haven't got it,' he mumbled; 'I swapped Ned Potter.'

'Well, can I have a look at your swap then?' she asked.

'I didn't get a comic.'

'What did you get?'

'Oh – nothing.'

'You must have got something.'

He did not explain or argue further and Mary Ann's attention was drawn away from him, for the clock made a sound like a hiccup as it always did when it passed the six. It was half past five. She looked towards the door, waiting and listening; her mother went on sewing, not lifting her head; and Michael continued to gaze into the fire.

The seconds ticked by, getting louder and slower in her ears, and just a small tremor of panic seized her when she found herself counting them. She had counted sixty eleven times when she rose from the fender. Their Michael was still staring into the fire and her ma was still sewing. She went and stood by the table, still counting. She counted sixty twice more, then she attempted to speak, but she got a frog in her throat and she croaked instead. It would have been funny at any other time, but not now.

When her throat was clear she asked, 'Can I go down to the front door, Ma?'

'No,' said Lizzie.

She stood staring at her mother, whose face seemed the same colour as her hair. Then she looked at the clock. It said a quarter to six. Well, he could have lost the bus – there were hundreds and hundreds of workmen waiting near the Mercantile for the buses. The feeling of panic swelled. Not on a Saturday though.

Then her mother spoke the words that sent the panic swirling through her body. Lizzie had risen from her chair and was folding up the mending, and she said, 'Come and get your tea.'

'No, no, not yet – oh, not yet.'

'There's no use waiting.' Her mother moved about the room as she spoke.

'Just a few minutes more – oh, Ma!'

'Now stop it!' Lizzie's voice was sharp as she turned on her, but it immediately softened as she said, 'It's no use.'

What was no use wasn't explained, and they looked at

each other until Mary Ann's head sank, and, moving a step to the side, she slid on to her chair. Her mother then said, 'Michael.' But Michael's answer was to screw himself farther round until his face was hidden completely from them.

Lizzie passed a hand over her brow. She looked from the back of her son to the face of her daughter. If there were only Michael she knew what she would do – pack up this minute and go. And when he came rolling in at eleven o'clock, then perhaps he'd believe what she said. But there was her. She'd never get her away from the house no matter what ruse she used.

'Start your tea.'

'I don't want any.'

'Now do what you're told. Michael . . . come along.'

The boy did not move, and she went to him and, taking his arm, led him to the table.

With her eyes Mary Ann watched her mother mash the tea but with her ears she was trying to separate the sounds of the house and leave a wide space for the sound for which she was waiting. The clock said six, then five past, then ten past, and she still had her first piece of tea-cake on her plate. Michael across from her was eating slowly and stubbornly, and suddenly she had a deep concern for him as she had for her da. She thought, Oh don't let him cry, for if he cries he'll be wild at himself; and the blame would be her da's, and Michael would hate him more.

By half past six the panic feeling had given place to the awfulness, which was how she described to herself the anxiety, the fear and the love which combined to cause the feeling of utter sadness.

'Are you finished?'

'What?' Mary Ann blinked at her mother – she had been brought back from her listening. 'I mean – pardon?'

'Are you finished?'

'Yes.' They had all been finished a long time.

'Then say your Grace.'

'Bless us, O Lord, and these Thy gifts, which we have received through Thy bounty. Through Christ, our Lord, A—' She stopped. There were thundering footsteps on the stairs, not sick footsteps and yet not her da's usual steps. They sounded like someone bounding up the stairs two at a time.

All their eyes were on the door when it burst open, and Mike Shaughnessy came into the room, red of face and laughing . . . and sober.

'Da, oh Da.' She was hanging on to his arm, jumping up and down like a Jack-in-the-box, and he said, 'Here, here. Hold on. Stop it. Look, you'll have old Miss Harper's ceiling down.'

He looked from her to Lizzie. 'I'm sorry I'm late,' he said.

Lizzie stared at him, her face a mixture of relief and astonishment.

'You'll never guess what happened.' He moved towards her, and her head moved slightly.

'I got an accumulator up.'

'An accumulator?' Only her lips showed that she was repeating the word.

'I took a chance and backed Bird's Eye. It was a rank outsider in the two-thirty. I put ten shillings on. Yes I know, I know.' He quelled the protest in her eyes. 'But it came off. It was ten to one and the lot went on to Fancy Fair, and, God alive, that came up and then every penny was on Raindrop. It was the favourite and only two to one. If it had been anything of a price . . . Liz, don't cry. Aw, I knew what you'd be thinking, but I wanted to come home with the money, and I had to wait until the Anchor opened and Reg Brown paid out – I was afraid he might skedaddle with that lot – but I didn't even. . . .' He paused, and suddenly Liz sat down and dropped her face into her hands.

'Ma, don't.' Michael was on one side of her and Mary Ann on the other and Mike in front, and Michael repeated again, 'Oh Ma, don't.'

Mike said nothing, but drew her hands from her face and, taking a wad of notes from his pocket, he closed her fingers about them.

The tears dropping on their joined hands, she looked down on the notes.

'There's over thirty there. I've kept three, and no one's going to stop me from spending them.' He took hold of her chin, lifting her face up to him. 'We're all going to Newcastle.'

Lizzie could only blink and say, 'It's too late.'

'It's not too late.'

'You haven't had your tea.'

'All I want is a wash.'

'But—'

'Ma, Ma, come on.' Mary Ann pulled at her mother's arm, and even Michael added to her entreaty and said, 'Let's go, Ma.'

'Where's that water?' Mike swung round and Mary Ann dashed to the fire and lifted the kettle from the hob and had the water in a dish by the time her da had stripped himself to the waist. She watched him lather his hair, and when he gave a particular grunt she lifted an enamel jug of cold water, and as she poured it over his head, turning his thick hair into spirals of rust-coloured ringlets, her thoughts too flowed with it like benediction, bathing him with her admiration and love.

CHAPTER FOUR

THE BLINDNESS OF FATHER OWEN

WHY was it, Mary Ann wondered, that happiness lasted for only short periods whereas unhappiness seemed to go on for ever? or was it, she pondered, that unhappiness was made of stronger stuff than happiness? It must be something like that, for she could recall vividly the numerous times she had been unhappy, yet when she tried to recall the happy times the memories were weak and elusive, like the vapour that floated over the river; she couldn't pin them down. Even that wonderful week-end when her da had won all that money and had taken them to Newcastle, that seemed now like something she had seen at the pictures, it wasn't real; yet it had happened only four weeks ago.

The week-end following it had promised to be the same, too, but her grannie had stepped in and spoilt it. Oh, how she hated her grannie. Why hadn't she said 'Milk bottles!' to stop her. But it would have been no use saying 'Milk bottles' or trying any other means of stopping her grannie that time. It had all happened on a Sunday. Her ma had taken her and Michael down to their grannie's in the afternoon because their da was at work, and Mr. Quinton was there, and her grannie had a fancy tea all set out in the front room. And then Michael had made them all laugh, except, of course, her grannie, by saying for his Grace 'Oh Lord, make us able to eat all that's on the table.' She could remember being amazed at their Michael making anyone laugh; but since their da had been working overtime and hadn't been – sick, Michael had been different, even to their da. And all this had made their ma look really like a girl again, especially with the new dress and coat her da had bought her for her birthday. She herself hadn't been able to buy that frock she had set her heart on for her ma, although she had looked out for courting couples until she was tired. She had even got a clip on the ear off one girl who was having a row with her lad up a back lane off Ferry Street. It had been no use trying to explain she was only listening so as to be able to help.

But it didn't matter now, nothing seemed to matter any more since that Sunday night. She had become deader and deader inside since then. If she could feel mad, or scream or cry, it would be better than this feeling that made her want to die. She had actually been praying to the Holy Family for them to make her die this last week, and all through her grannie.

The scene, like all unhappy things, was held fast in her mind and she couldn't get rid of it. She had only to shut her eyes to see it all as plain as plain. They were having their tea and her ma was laughing at something funny Mr. Quinton had said, when her da walked in. For a moment he had looked terrifying as he glared down on Mr. Quinton, then he had laughed and said something to her grannie about when she was making plans she should always be prepared for setbacks. Mr. Quinton had got up from the table and stared back at her da, but he hadn't spoken to him. Then he said good-bye to her grannie and her ma and he had called her ma Elizabeth, and when he had gone her da had said, 'And now E-liz-a-beth, with your mother's permission, we will go home. It seems a great pity I was finished early, I spoilt the party. And your mother must have gone to great pains to organize it.' Then he had suddenly dropped his quiet voice and, turning on her grannie, had cried, 'You old devil, you!'

After that she couldn't really remember what was said, except the feeling of terror her grannie's admission had brought to her, for her grannie had said she would go on planning until she had her daughter away from him. She could recall the terrifying stillness of the room and then her da saying, 'But what about a divorce? There's no divorce for a Catholic, is there? If your plan worked out you'd be making her live in sin, wouldn't you? You old hypocrite.'

On this her ma had got them all out of the house and they had come back to Jarrow, and no one spoke at all on the way until they got home; and then her da wouldn't believe that her ma didn't know Mr. Quinton was going to be at her grannie's, and they fought in the bedroom, a different kind of fighting, talking low and quiet and bitterly. And at intervals during the following week they had talked like that. But still her da hadn't been sick until last Saturday, and even then he hadn't meant to be, for he had come in at half past five after doing overtime, and it was then her ma had told him she'd had the offer of a house, one of the newer ones, up Primrose Way. At first he had been pleased, and then he had begun to question her, and in a sudden burst of temper her ma had admitted it was through Mr. Quinton's influence that the offer had been made. Her da had gone out then and got sick, not blind sick but just sick enough to talk and talk and talk; and twice during the week he had gone and got sick like that again; and last night as she held the towel for him he asked her quite suddenly 'Do you like Mr. Quinton?' and she had lied promptly, saying, 'No, no, I hate him.' And as he dried himself he had said flatly, 'You can't lie to me – you like him because he's smart and has a fine big car and he never swears.'

'I don't.'

'And what's more, he doesn't get – sick – does he?'

She had fallen against him and clung to his leg and he had said something to himself that made her shiver. 'Life's hell,'

56

he had said. He had loosened her hands from him and walked away. There seemed to be a deadness about him – he didn't bounce or rush or laugh any more – and the deadness was on her too, and she wished that she was really dead – dead as dead and in purgatory, and so taken up with going through it for her sins that she wouldn't have time to feel like this.

'If I have to speak to you again, Mary Ann Shaughnessy, you'll know about it. Are you going to confession?'

'Yes, oh yes, Miss Johnson.' Mary Ann dragged herself up out of her misery and from her desk.

'Then stop dreaming. ... Now you'll all walk three abreast, and if there's any carry-on in the street like there was last Thursday you'll all be for it in the morning. Grace Smith, stop that pushing there. ... All those going to Father Beaney at the front and those for Father Owen at the back here.'

Mary Ann joined the latter group. Not only did she not scramble for the front place but she took the inner side of the last three in the ranks which ensured her the unenviable position of being the last to go into confession, but that was what she wanted, for when she was last she could talk to her heart's content and the priest wouldn't hurry her on. Once she had told Father Owen all that was on her mind she knew that she would get some relief from this feeling. She had seen him a number of times during the past week but of course she couldn't tell him her trouble in any other place but the confessional box, for she didn't want him to know it was she who was troubled, or what she was troubled by, and in the confessional box he wouldn't know it was her, for as everybody knew God struck priests blind once they entered their part of the box so that they wouldn't know who was talking. They might peer through the grid but they couldn't see a styme. That's why you could tell them everything that was in your heart and not be afraid they'd split on you.

57

As the crocodile swung out of the school-yard it touched on a group of the bigger girls. They, too, were on their way to confession, but, because of their years, free and unhampered, and among them and near to Mary Ann's side of the ranks was Sarah Flannagan.

After mimicking the marching by striding along the gutter swinging her arms, Sarah addressed herself to Mary Ann's averted face and hissed, 'Convict!' whereupon Mary Ann, without turning her head but mouthing each syllable widely, said, 'Cas-i-bi-anca, flannel face!'

This retort had the effect of infuriating Sarah and with her fist she pushed Mary Ann in the back and knocked her flying into the girl in front, who, in turn, fell on to the girl in front of her. The result was four children lying on the pavement and Miss Johnson standing over them, saying, 'Who did this?'

There was a chorus of 'Mary Ann Shaughnessy, miss.'

'It wasn't!' Mary Ann denied emphatically. 'It was Sarah Flannagan.'

But since there was neither sight nor sound of Sarah Flannagan Miss Johnson said, 'You come to me tomorrow morning,' which added bitterness to Mary Ann's collection of negative feelings and a new resentment against so-called justice.

In church she found it impossible to make her preparation for confession – she could only keep thinking that she wished she were dead. With one thing and another, she was fed-up and tired of it all. If only it was possible to die quickly – like that. She snapped her finger and thumb against her bent forehead. If something could happen and she could be struck dead. Laurie Carter had said her mother knew a man who had been struck dead because he swore at a priest. ... She lifted her eyes over the back rest and looked across the church to where the Holy Family were enthroned in deep shadow. If she was struck dead she'd likely go straight to them. For the moment she had forgotten the required passage through purgatory. Suppose she swore at Father Owen. Eeh, what had put that into her head? Fancy thinking about swearing at Father Owen! But if it would make her die . . . No, not Father Owen. Well, which other priest did she know but Father Beaney? and she wouldn't have the courage to go up to Father Beaney and swear at him. She stared through the dimness towards the altar, and presently she thought, 'If I'm going to do it, Father Owen will be the best.' Suppose, as she was kneeling in the box, she did just a little swear at him. Perhaps that would do, and when he died he'd know she hadn't meant it. But what should she swear? Should she say damn? No, that wasn't quite big enough. Bloody? Eeh! no, that was too awful. She might be sent to Hell for ever for that.

The last penitent came stumbling out of the box, and rising from her knees, she sent up a quick prayer to the Holy Family in an appeal to be provided with the swear words necessary to cause her demise. She groped her way into the dark confessional and knelt down below the grid and began in her customary way, 'Pray Father give me thy blessing for I have sinned. It is a week since my last confession.'

'Yes. Go on.' The priest's voice seemed to come from a great distance and did not for the moment seem to be the soothing voice of Father Owen but of a priest who already knew all her sins and the blackness of her heart, so, quickly, she gathered her wits together and presented them to him, 'Please, Father, I have given way to the sin of hate.'

'Who do you hate?'

'Me grannie.'

'Why?'

'Well, she's always saying nasty things about me da and she wants me ma to leave him and she's got another man all ready for her. The other man's nice enough but he's not me da.'

There was a movement of the priest's feet, and he said, 'Your mother – what does she say about all this?'

'Nothing, Father – at least they fight a bit. She gets sick to the heart because he goes and gets a skinful. I mean he gets drunk.'

There, she had said the word. It was only in here in the fast secretness of this box with this blind priest that she could utter that word.

'When was he last drunk?'

'He had a few last night, Father.'

'Go on with your confession.'

'I've kicked our—' She stopped herself saying the word Michael, he might recognize her through that name; so she said, 'Me brother. And I've torn up the scraps of paper he writes on, and made him wild by calling him Ginger. And I've missed my morning prayers because I got up late, and I've looked over Cissy Tollard's shoulder into her exercise book.'

'Yes; go on.'

She was raking round in her mind for her other great sins when it came back to her that not a few minutes ago she had committed the worst sin of all by deciding to swear at him.

'Go on, my child.'

But she couldn't go on. And after waiting a while he said, 'Come on, my child, finish your confession.'

'I wanted . . .'

'Yes?' he encouraged.

'In the church, a minute back, I made up my mind to swear at you, Father.'

'You what?'

Two white bulbs came close to the grid and looked down on Mary Ann, but she looked fearlessly back into them knowing that the eyes were sightless. After a while they were withdrawn and the priest said, 'And why did you want to swear at me?'

' 'Cause I wanted to die.'

'Because you wanted to die?' There was utter bewilderment in his tone.

'Yes, I heard tell that if you swore at a priest you'd be struck down dead.'

Father Owen gave two short coughs, then he blew his nose before saying, 'And why, may I ask, do you want to die?'

'I told you, Father, it's about me da. I'm miserable and I never want me dinner and I don't care if I can go out to play or not. I even thought if I could find some poison I'd take it and when I was dead me da might be sorry and not get drunk again.'

'Poison?' The priest's voice was crisp now. 'Poison's no use, I've tried it.'

'You have, Father?' She was brought clean out of her own trouble with surprise and she stretched up to see better into the dimness beyond the grid.

'Yes, it only gives you the gripes in your inside and you're no better off.'

'Oh—' The thought of gripes in her inside turned her for ever from the thought of poison, but she went on, warming up to the situation, 'Last night I was so miserable, Father, and me ma wouldn't let me go out and look for me da and I thought if I could get out I'd a good mind to throw meself under the bus where it rounds the Ben Lomond in Ellison Street.'

'Under a bus? Oh, that's a worse idea altogether.'

'Is it, Father?'

'I'd say it is. What happens when you throw yourself under a bus? It chops off either your arms or your legs and you live on, and it's not a very pleasant state having no arms or legs, is it?'

'No, Father.'

'Well, forget about the bus, and pray to the. . . . Who do you usually pray to?'

'To the Holy Family, Father.'

'Oh, the Holy Family ... well, you couldn't pray to a better Family, and you pray to them tonight and ask them for something nice to happen to you. What would you like to happen?'

'Oh, Father. For me da ... '

'Oh' – he cut her short – 'leave your da to God. Now isn't there something you want to happen to yourself?'

'Well, I wanted to get into the procession, Father.'

'And you're not in it?'

'No, Father, and all of them have been picked.'

'Yes. . . . Ah well, you go on praying to the Holy Family and you can be assured they'll make something nice happen to you.'

'They will, Father?'

'They will that. They never fail. Now for your penance say the first Joyful Mystery of the Rosary, and make your act of contrition.'

'O my God, I am very sorry I have sinned against Thee because Thou art so good, and by the help of Thy Holy Grace I will never sin again.'

'Good night and God bless you.'

'Good night, Father.'

Out of the confessional box, Mary Ann decided it would not be wise to stay in a now empty church to say her penance, for the priest, once out of the box and his sight back, would know it was her he had been talking to. And he'd remember about the drink and connect it with her da.

On the way home she wondered what nice thing the Holy Family would make happen to her; but this only played on the fringe of her thoughts, for deep in the permanency of her mind she knew there was only one thing that really mattered, one thing that would make her happy, and that was the happiness of her ma and da.

Friday was usually a nice day. It began by having your breakfast packed up and going off to Communion, then going straight to school and eating your breakfast in the hall, that's if you hadn't already eaten it on the road. Then there was Bible History, and one Friday in every four Father Owen or Father Beaney came and heard your Catechism. It was nice on the days Father Owen came, for he made you laugh. Then the class acted pages from history – today it was to be Flora Macdonald and Bonnie Prince Charlie. And in the afternoon there was the poetry lesson. She liked poetry and could remember long bits of it. When she was in Miss Harrington's class she used to get pennies for being the first to learn, but Miss Johnson didn't give you anything . . . only the stick if you didn't know it. But she never got the stick for not knowing her poetry. She knew long stretches of Hiawatha's childhood. It was easy stuff to learn because the man who wrote it kept repeating everything so as to make it easy to remember like:

> 'He was a marvellous story-teller,
> He was a traveller and a talker,
> He was a friend of old Nokomis,
> Made a bow for Hiawatha;
> From a branch of ash he made it,
> From an oak-bough made the arrows,
> Tipped with flint, and winged with feathers . . .'

Oh, she knew yards and yards of it.

> 'I have given you streams to fish in,
> I have given you bear and bison,
> I have given you roe and reindeer,
> I have given you brant and beaver . . .'

Sometimes at night she put herself to sleep saying it.

Yes, she usually liked Fridays, at school anyway, but to-day the misery from last night still lay heavily upon her. She had arrived home from Confession to find her ma out, and she hadn't got back before her da came in, and they didn't speak. And he'd gone out after he'd had his tea and got a little sick; and in the night she had woken up on the camp bed where she slept under the sloping roof by the side of the scullery door and there, lying on the mat in front of the dead fire, was her da, with just a blanket over him. She felt so bad at the sight of him lying there in the cold that she began to cry. She had got up and the noise she caused brought her ma out of the room, and she made her get back into bed. And now here she was in school, with her breakfast still uneaten, and feeling more than ever that she wanted to die.

This morning was Catechism test and all the partitions of the school had been pushed back and Father Owen was up now on the platform talking. She wasn't paying much attention to him, for she was having her work cut out to keep her six inches of bottom space on the edge of the desk seat. All about her was a mass of heads and shoulders, except to the right of her where there was a little altar. It was St. Anthony's altar, and he was standing on a pedestal in his brown habit with no shoes on, and his feet looked cold, she thought, and there were bits of dirt in between his toes. In a detached way she decided that when she was moved up into this class after the summer holidays she'd scrape out all that dirt. She didn't like dirt between her toes – her ma made her and Michael wash their feet every night before they went to bed. They were a rare family for washing, especially her da. The thought of her da brought back the thought of dying, and she looked once again at St. Anthony. She had never laid much stock by him, yet she heard he was quite good at finding things for you if you lost them. She wondered, if she prayed to him now, how long he would take to bring about her wish. Anyway, it would pass the time away for there was nothing to see in front of her and nothing to hear but a mumbling of voices.

There had been quite a big stir at the beginning of pro-
ceedings because Betty Paul, who was to lead the procession
dressed in a blue cloak and a crown like Our Lady, had gone
and got the measles. Fancy anybody going and getting the
measles when they were going to lead the May Procession
and walk bang behind the statue of Our Lady hoisted on a
platform and carried by four boys. She wouldn't have done a
silly thing like that. But what did it matter, she wanted to
die.

She looked up into the face of St. Anthony and with first a
little placation just to soothe him and make up for her neglect
of him, she began, 'Dear St. Anthony, I haven't prayed to
you because I've been so busy, but I know full well how
clever you are, and you could perform any miracle you like if
you wanted to. Dear St. Anthony, I'm very miserable, and
you being in Heaven will know why. And please, St.
Anthony I want to die, oh, I want to die. I can't bear to
think about me da. . . .'

'Mary Ann Shaughnessy – where is she?'

The priest's voice was lost to her, but a thump between
the shoulders was an effective way of recalling her to it. A
number of voices hissed at her 'Go on out.' 'Are you daft?'
'Don't you hear Father Owen calling you?' 'What's up with
her?' The voices brought her to her feet and she looked
towards the platform, and there was Father Owen laughing
and beckoning to her with his hand.

'Come on, come on, Mary Ann,' he called. 'Were you
asleep?'

As dazed as if she had been, she walked towards the platform wondering all the while what she had done to be called
out. Surely it wasn't because of last night – she was going to
report to Miss Johnson when her class assembled again. Her
teacher was at the bottom of the steps, but said nothing to
her, only pushed her up them, and not too gently either, and
still in a daze, Mary Ann found herself in front of Father

Owen and with a whole sea of faces around her, for on the platform was the headmistress and a lot of the teachers, and not one of them was looking pleasant.

What had she done to be brought up here? Only if you stole anything or broke somebody's windows were you yanked up on the platform and made an example of.

'Well, there it is. One person's bad luck is another's good.' Father Owen put his hand on Mary Ann's head and slowly screwed her around to face the school. 'As I've already said, nobody was more upset than myself when I knew that Betty had the measles and I had to find someone to take her place, so, as it is my privilege to pick from the school the leader of the procession, I have decided on Mary Ann Shaughnessy here. Granted Mary Ann is small' – he looked down on her – 'but I've a notion that the Holy Mother herself was a slight body, and the gown may have to be shortened, but that can easily be done. I have chosen her because there is no black mark against her in school, and since she made her first confession fifteen months ago there has not been one week but she has attended Confession and Communion. Now let us give her a great big clap.'

He led the clapping by banging his long bony hands together. Mary Ann gazed up at him, then at the obedient clapping hands in front of her, then to the side where the teachers were clapping in such a way that would not have disturbed a sleeping baby, and she asked herself whether she was in bed having another of her dreams. But no, she wasn't, for her eyes were on a level with the bottom button of Father Owen's slack waistcoat and she could feel his fingers moving in her hair. She was just about to realize the wonderful enormity of the thing that was happening to her when out of the blue came the answer to her eager prayer of a moment ago. She felt it first starting in her legs as a shooting pain which screwed itself up through her chest and into her head. All the faces about her began to run into one. She made a great effort to steady herself and to keep her feet on the ground but it was no use, and when, without any warning, Father Owen's long thin figure began to swell before her eyes she knew, in an illuminating flash, what was happening – her earnest prayer to the Saint was being answered and she was about to die. The inadvisability of dealing with two firms for the one product was brought home to her – competition could evoke disastrous results. The efficacy of St. Anthony's power was terrifying – he was as sharp as the Devil himself. She spun round to where his statue showed dimly in the distance, and there he stood laughing at her – she could hear him. She turned about to where the statue of Our Lady dominated the side wall above the platform and cried, 'Put it right with him, will you? I don't want to die now . . . well not just yet.'

But neither the Virgin nor the complete Holy Family had anything, it would appear, on St. Anthony for quick service, for he strode from his pedestal shouting, 'It's nice to be able to play God,' and he picked her up in his arms and carried her off and rushed her straight through the air heaven-wards.

The rush of the air made her gasp and his voice boomed in her ears as he shouted from the clouds down to the head-mistress, 'I consider her need the greatest.'

Suddenly he dropped her and she gasped and gasped for breath as she fell. Having landed with a thump, she opened her eyes; then after one startled glance about her she lay back in contentment as she realized she was in the sanctuary of the Teachers' Room, lying on a couch, with the Head-mistress on one side of her and Father Owen on the other.

'You're feeling better? That's it. Ah – that's it. You've been to Communion and haven't eaten your breakfast, I bet. Now, am I right?'

She made a slight movement with her head and he laughed and said, 'I knew it.'

'Father.'

'Yes?'

'It's true . . . about . . . ?'

'You going to lead the procession?'

She nodded again.

'As true as life, but only if you drink a glass of hot milk and eat up a good breakfast.'

'I'm not going to die?'

'Die?' His long body seemed to fold up with laughter. 'I should say not. And you're going to wear that lovely blue gown.'

She gazed up at him. He didn't know it was her he had told last night to pray for something nice to happen, and she couldn't tell him for it would give the show away. But lifting her hands, she caught hold of his fingers and pressed them to her cheek. 'Oh, Father, Father,' she said.

CHAPTER FIVE

MR. FLANNAGAN, THE CORONATION, AND MIKE SHAUGHNESSY

NOWHERE in Jarrow was the Coronation looked forward to and prepared for more than in Burton Street. For weeks there had been Committee Meetings. That the Committee grew in numbers and became divided in policy was to be expected, but that the divided parties should break up within themselves into smaller factions was to be regretted. Some were for teas in the street with games afterwards for the bairns, some, remembering rain-soaked street parties from the past, were all for the Baptists' Hall; but as Mrs. McBride said, who'd want to get drunk in the Baptists' Hall? This called down censure from most of the factions. Who wanted to get drunk at all? Those who wanted that kind of a party had better take themselves down to the Fifteen Streets and not join in the festivities of a respectable neighbourhood. There was a nodding of heads and the murmuring of the name of Shaughnessy. Then there were those who suggested that every adult in the street should subscribe five shillings, the accumulated wealth to be used for sending three of them, these to be determined by a draw, up to London to see the actual procession. Before protests could rain down on this proposal it was haughtily thrust aside by Mrs. Flannagan saying that if the Flannagans wanted to go to London they were quite able to provide their own train fare, thank you, and they had already refused the offer to accompany her sister and husband from Hartlepools who were going to her sister's husband's cousin and he had an excellent view already for them, from the window of the office where he worked, slap on the Coronation route.

At this, a combined murmur like the wash of the tide on a pebble beach came from all quarters, and it could have been translated into 'Oh ye-ah!'

Finally, after many meetings, a street party was decided upon, which as some of the Committee said, had been inevitable from the first. One stipulation was made: should it rain the bairns were to have their tea in the Baptists' Hall and Mr. Gallon engaged to do his Punch and Judy Show. Of course there was one snag here, as those people who were not tired of arguing pointed out, they couldn't leave it until June 2nd to say if it was going to rain before engaging Mr. Gallon – he'd have to be engaged wet or dry.

The day dawned and it does not need testifying that it was wet, but it took more than rain to damp the enthusiasm of the tenants of Burton Street and Mulhattans' Hall in particular. The children were wild with excitement, and the adults got rid of much of their suppressed emotion in trying to quell the exuberance of their young.

But put two hundred and twenty-six people in a hall that would be crowded with half that number and you will find all emotions subsidiary to the feeling of self-preservation. So at least thought Mike Shaughnessy.

He was sober and dressed in his best and standing in the corner of the hall. It would have been impossible to sit down had there been anything to sit on. The only advantage he had was his view – his head topped every other man's and woman's in the room – and he looked down on the rows of trestle tables lined with children and the rows of their admiring parents watching them eating as if they were accomplishing the feat for the first time in their lives.

Mike was not unaware that he was a subject of interest;

that he was sober on such a day as this was a source of wonder to his neighbours. From different quarters he had seen covert glances and heard whispered words. At least he was a man who wasn't unknown. He smiled wryly to himself as his eyes roamed over the crowd, halting here and there to hold a gaze fixed on him in curiosity, and he wondered if anyone in this room would believe that ten years ago he hadn't known the taste of beer or whisky. Yes, there was one ... she knew.

His eyes went to Lizzie. It was easy for him to find her, for he hadn't allowed her to move far from his sight all afternoon. She was like a queen among peasants, standing out far above them. My God, if ever there was a fool in this world he was one – to exchange her for a skinful of beer! He could only blame himself, not Quinton. He would lose her; then what would become of him? He'd be finished. Why did he do it? Why wasn't he as big and tough inside as he was out? Why did the smell of oil and tar and rope and the singey smell of hot rivets fill his stomach with the craving? Yet it was no use blaming the work and the sweat; he recalled the periods when he had sweated on the land. He had burned then for a drink, but a draught of spring water or a canful of milk had swilled it away. He was weak and he knew it.

It seemed like the twisting that Fate was apt to indulge in that he couldn't settle on a farm away from her and the youngsters, yet if she left him and he was adrift with nothing to hold him to this blasted town he would still be unable to return to the land. She mustn't leave him ... ever. His heart began to beat rapidly, pumping as if at the end of a run, and he felt his pulse beat, as it had often seemed to do of late, in his eyes. Just the thought of losing her filled him with the terror of loneliness, that loneliness that he had known as a child and then as a boy, the loneliness that made him shun crowds and people, the loneliness that for its easing required only one heart to beat against. If she left him, the loneliness

71

he had known before would be as nothing to what would
come in the years ahead. But it needn't happen. It was up to
him; he had only to go steady. She didn't mind him having a
glass or two if he could stop at that. Yes, if he could. And
then there was the other one tugging at the secret place in his
heart. If anyone could keep a man straight it should be that
child. His son, he knew, wouldn't care if he was gone the
morrer, but Mary Ann. . . . He looked towards her and her
eyes were waiting for him. She waved her hand and he
waved back. The pride of him showed in her face, and he
thought that she could be proud at any rate of her achieve-
ment in getting him here today. God knew she had worked
hard enough at it, but he did not know for how much longer
he could stand this crush and the warm, damp air of the
room. The noise was a bedlam vying with that of the dry-
dock, and he was feeling it pressing down on him. If only he
could make his way towards that door and stand in the street
a moment and get himself a mouthful of air. Judiciously he
began to edge his way forward. He even got past the entrance
to the hall kitchen where plates and trays were being handed
overhead from hand to hand, but just beyond this and within
a few steps of the door his progress was halted and he found
himself wedged in another corner to make room for the hasty
exit of a child who had eaten well but not wisely. She was
being pushed through the crowd with the fiercesome admon-
ition from her mother to 'Hold it.' The dire penalty of her
refusing to comply with this order rose above the clamour.
The situation amused Mike and he laughed, and so did the
man at his side, and Mike turned his head towards him and
said, 'Poor little beggar, she's between the devil and the deep
sea.' The man looked back at him for a moment without
speaking, then he laughed again, but not such a hearty laugh
this time and said, 'Yes. Yes, you're right.'

'And,' commented Mike to himself, 'you're another poor
little devil.' Anyone unfortunate enough to have to spend a

lifetime with that upstart woman Flannagan had his sympathy. Mike chuckled inwardly. How often had he been threatened that he would suffer for his insolence at the hands of this little chap, and up to the present this was the nearest they had got to each other.

He said quite pleasantly, 'I'm trying to make for the door to get some air,' and Mr. Flannagan replied with equal pleasantness, 'I'm heading that way meself.'

They nodded at each other, a strange, comradely nod that said, 'We may as well make it together then.'

'London's got nothing on this,' said Mike, when at last the double doors were reached.

'You're right there, Mr. Shaughnessy.'

Oh, thought Mike, we're getting our title the day – Mr. Shaughnessy it is. And to think we've seen each other every day for two years with never a 'Whatcher there!'

'Harry!' The astonished, strident voice brought Mr. Flannagan swiftly round and he stood with his back to the door and faced his wife. 'Where you off to?'

Mr. Flannagan did not answer for a moment, but his eyes flitted to Mike's back where he stood struggling with the long iron bar of the door. Then he said briefly, 'Outside.'

'Why?' asked Mrs. Flannagan. 'What do you want to go outside for?'

Mr. Flannagan's answer to this was drowned by Mike's laugh. Perhaps he was laughing at himself being unable to get the door open. With a quick jerk the bar went upwards and the double doors shot apart, and as he turned to close them his eyes met the malevolent glare of Mrs. Flannagan, and he laughed in her face and closed the door on her words, 'Stay where you are till the air's clearer.'

Mike stood in the shelter of the porch for a moment and looked at the rain falling like a solid lead sheet across the opening, and Mrs. Flannagan's voice, muffled now but still audible, came to him. He could not distinguish what she was

73

saying but her tone told him that the poor little devil was getting it hot and heavy. As the door behind him opened again he turned his collar up and stepped out into the rain. He found it was not amusing to hear the little fellow being slated; rather, he was embarrassed. When a woman made a man look small it touched all men.

'Do you hear me?' Mrs. Flannagan's voice followed him through the opened door. Then on a pitch of a scream it came down the empty street, crying, 'Harry!' and it told Mike that Mr. Flannagan must be somewhere behind him. He did not turn round, but he thought with a glow of satisfaction, 'So he stood his ground ... good for him.' And he slowed his pace until the little man came abreast. The odd thing was that Mr. Flannagan made no effort to pass on, but suited his steps to Mike's, having to lengthen his stride to do so. This must have conveyed the worst to Mrs. Flannagan, for her voice crying, 'Do you hear me, Harry Flannagan? Come back here this minute!' seemed to hit the two men in the neck. Anyway, it sent them forward at a quicker pace until they rounded the corner of the street. There Mr. Flannagan, his face running with rain, looked up at Mike and asked quite solemnly, 'Would you mind me company, Mr. Shaughnessy?' and Mike, successfully keeping his eyebrows stationary, replied in his politest tone, 'Not at all, Mr. Flannagan, not at all.'

*   *   *

Mary Ann saw her da leave the hall, and for a moment the brightness of this wonderful day vanished, until she told herself that he had only gone out for a mouthful of air and he would be back in a minute. But he didn't come back in a minute.

The tea over, the children were bidden to sit where they were to see the Punch and Judy Show. Mary Ann tried to catch her mother's eye and ask her permission to attempt to

74

leave the table, but Lizzie's eyes seemed to rest everywhere but on her daughter. Mary Ann did not care for Punch and Judy – the sight of poor Judy being beaten unmercifully with a stick always made her close her eyes – so at this point in the entertainment she followed the ruse of so many other children who were bored with sitting in one spot for so long, she put up her hand. It seemed to her that almost immediately her mother was behind her, and with a warning injunction for quiet, she lifted her off the form and carried her with some difficulty through the press, but not towards the backyard of the hall, but to the main door. Once outside, she put her down, saying, 'There are too many waiting, we'd better go home.' She did not say, 'You had better run home and then come back,' and Mary Ann knew that her ma wanted to go and see if her da was home.

It had stopped raining now and they hurried along hand in hand. Mulhattans' Hall was quiet and had the air of a house that had been vacated in a hurry, especially in the hallway outside Mrs. McBride's door, for there reposed a welter of oddments, the possessions undoubtedly of Mrs. McBride's numerous grandchildren. Mary Ann ran ahead up the stairs and pushed open their door.

She did not call down to her mother that her da wasn't in, but her silence was telling enough for Lizzie, and when she entered the room she made no comment one way or the other but an anger rose in her against the man who was so weak and so selfish that he would not keep his promise to this child even for a day. The promise had not been given in words; but in a thousand and one ways Mary Ann had tried to impress on him the importance of Coronation Day and extract from him a laugh or the slow shaking of the head or a quick hoist in the air, and all these she took as signs that he would stay with them on that day and enter into the jollification.

Her own heart had softened towards him as it hadn't done

for some time when she had seen him standing patiently with the crowd in the hall, for she knew how human contact in the mass could irritate him. But it had been too much for him. She had expected too much of him. Her anger made her silently vehement. He was weak, he was cowardly, he was rotten to the core. Let him hurt her, she could in a way stand up to it, but the look on the child's face when yet once again he had let her down was heart-rending. She turned to Mary Ann who was standing near the table picking at her fingers and said, 'I thought you wanted to leave the room?'

'I did.' Mary Ann turned and walked out and down the stairs, and Lizzie went into the scullery, and after staring down into the sink for some time she beat her fist three times in quick succession on the draining-board, and when the sound of Mary Ann's footsteps mounting the stairs again came to her she sighed heavily and went into the kitchen, and with an effort towards brightness she greeted her daughter, 'Well, shall we go back?'

'No, I don't want to.'

'Why?'

'Well, it will be nearly over.'

That was true. 'But,' said Lizzie, 'now that it's fair there'll be the races in the street and you've been practising for long enough.'

'I'm tired.'

'Now listen,' Lizzie spoke sharply. 'You're no more tired than I am,' which, if this had been strictly true, would have made Mary Ann very weary indeed.

'I am,' persisted Mary Ann, sitting down.

'What about the prizes you were after? The big box of chocolates Mr. Funnell's giving, and the doll to the best skipper?'

'I'm tired.'

Lizzie moved her head impatiently; then as a noise like a

stampede of cattle came from the street she said, 'There they are, all back.'

'I don't want to go.'

'But we were going to see all the bonfires later on – what about that?'

Mary Ann looked straight at her mother and the look said, 'If he comes in roarin' will we leave him and go and see the bonfires?'

Lizzie turned and went to the fireplace, and with the raker pulled from the back of the grate a little more coal on to the low embers, then swinging round almost fiercely, she cried, 'Well, you'll go to bed mind, I'm not having you sitting there with a face like that.'

Even this threat could not bring Mary Ann out of her misery, and when she said, 'All right', Lizzie gave her one helpless look before walking into the bedroom.

She sat on the edge of the bed and rocked herself slowly, Oh, dear God, dear God. Was this to be her life? There was no likelihood at all that he would return before he was well soaked, and he would say, 'Well now, take you for a spoil-sport. Isn't it every creature that's drinking the Queen's health the night?' His voice would be thick with the Irish brogue, a tongue she had come to detest, for the deeper his cup the thicker it came. Once he had tried to explain to her the reason why he spoke broad Irish when he was drunk. You've got to belong somewhere, he had said; there are two things a man must have, a mate and a country. When you grow up knowing that you belong to nowhere or to no one and that no one belongs to you, that your very name was given to you by a committee, and one name being as good as another, they let you be called after the man who had picked you up from the gate, when a thing like that is the kind of thought you live with from the time you start thinking you begin to make up places and people that do belong to you. It was natural I should pick on Ireland with a name like Mike

Shaughnessy, and for people it was as natural as breathing that I should pick on you the moment I saw you, with your golden hair and your promise of another world.

Oh, Mike, Mike. She leant her head on the bed-rail and her pity was resurrected. Why had life to be like this? Why wasn't she big enough to fill the loneliness that ate him up at times? He loved her, she was the only creature he wanted. He was capable of killing any man who would come between them, yet he could not kill or would not kill that which was a greater danger to their happiness than any man. Oh, Mike, Mike.

He had been gone three hours now. It would be another two or three before he would be back. She was weary and tired of thinking, tired of counting time, tired of worrying, tired of anxiety, tired of living. She raised her head and looked towards the window, for the noise and shouting from the street had suddenly increased. Was it only the echo of her worry or had she heard Mike's name called above the yelling and the shouting? She sat bolt upright, her ears strained. There it was again. Mike and Mr. Shaughnessy. Mr. Shaughnessy, the voice said.

Darting to the window she stopped and peered down into the street. The twilight had not yet deepened into darkness but the street lamps were lit and in the half-light she could not at first make out one figure from another; then her eyes were drawn over the crowd to a clearing, in the middle of which a man was dancing with his hands above his head. He was dancing a weird imitation of a Scotch reel, accompanied by the clapping and stamping of the crowd. But it was not Mike – it was Mr. Flannagan. She dropped on to her knees and lowered her head to the bottom of the window to confirm that she was seeing aright. It couldn't really be Mr. Flannagan, the solemn, miserable-looking little man, who rarely opened his mouth to anyone and was known never to have touched drink for years, not since he was converted to

78

sobriety by the visiting mission. Without closer confirmation she knew that only if he had ... 'had some' would he be dancing in the street. But Mike; they had been calling Mike. Where was he? Her eyes roamed wide over the crowd, peering through the distorted reflections of the lamps, only to come back to the cleared space. And then she saw him, and her amazement grew, for Mr. Flannagan, who had stopped dancing, was pulling him by the arm in an effort to induce him to join the fray.

That Mike should need inducement to join in a bit of jollification was a sure guarantee that he was sober. She was completely mystified by it all; everything was topsy-turvy, Mike sober and Mr. Flannagan drunk. Slowly she raised her eyes from the street to the window below on the far side of the road, and seeing the outline of Mrs. Flannagan's face behind the curtain and being only human, she voicelessly said, 'Now how do you like it, Mrs. Flannagan?' Then remembering the torture she herself had endured she added, 'But I wouldn't wish it on you, no matter what you're like.'

'Lizzie! Are you there, Lizzie?'

Lizzie turned from the window as Mrs. McBride's voice came from the other room; and before she could reach the door it was thrust open, and Fanny, puffing and yelling, cried, 'Was there ever such a crowning to a day as that? Have you seen him?'

She carried Lizzie towards the window again with a sweep of her arm. 'Look at him!' She pointed into the street. Then looking across to Mrs. Flannagan's window, she voiced the same sentiments as Lizzie had restrained. 'Ah, me fine madam. How d'you like it? This'll knock some of the stinking brag out of you. ... Oh' – she turned to Lizzie, her broad beaming smile making her face resemble nothing so much as a dented and rather discoloured bag of tripe – 'oh, if I've lived to see nothing else, this' – she indicated with a jerk of

79

her thumb the again dancing figure of Mr. Flannagan – 'this would have been worth all me struggles. And if it doesn't keep the Duchess of Dam' All quiet for the rest of her life I'm a Hallelujah. Oh, isn't Mike the boy that gets his own back! If he had tried for a thousand years he couldn't have thought of anything better.'

'Mike?' Lizzie looked at the old woman. 'What's Mike got to do with it?'

'He did it. Took him along and got him bottled up. Didn't you see them leaving the hall together? Mary Prout said there was a do in the street with Lady Golightly.'

Lizzie's face hardened as she stared down on to the back of Mrs. McBride's head. The things these people said. Mike had his faults, God knew, but petty vindictiveness was not one of them. Yet what about Mr. Flannagan trying to get him to dance? If they hadn't been together would he have done that?

'The street's alive with it,' went on Fanny, again cocking her head up to Lizzie. 'Everybody knows the things she's said about Mike. Aw, who says the devil doesn't look after his own? Do you want to look down, hinny?' She put her hand out to where Mary Ann was standing now near her mother. 'Come and see your da. He's down there as sober as a judge, and it's Coronation Day an' all.'

'I wouldn't say that, Fanny.'

The three of them turned abruptly to where Mike was filling the doorway. His face was not clearly discernible in the dimness of the room, but his voice, the inflection of which could tell Lizzie whether he had been on beer, whisky, or both, told her now that he'd had a few beers, but that was all.

'Oh, there you are, Mike. How did you get away from him? You've got yourself a drinking pal from now on. But what in the name of God gave you the idea? If you'd spat clean in her eye you wouldn't have hit her harder.'

As Fanny threw her laughing remarks to him, Mary Ann darted across the room. She did not shout, 'Da! Oh, Da!' but just clung on to his arm, pressing her face against his sleeve in a passionate expression of relief.

Mike fondled her head and asked of Fanny, 'Who says it was my idea getting him drunk?'

'Who says! ... Ah, what d'you take me for, Mike?' She pushed past him. 'Who says? Why everybody in the street, and they're all having a dam' good laugh, knowing the way she's held you up as a disgrace to the neighbourhood.'

'Has she now?'

'Has she now? Why are you playing so dumb all of a sudden? Has she now? Oh, you'll kill me with your fun one of these days. Well, here I am now going to see what happens when old Flannagan knocks on his door for admittance. I'll be seeing you, Lizzie. . . . Has she now?' She leered at Mike in farewell.

Lizzie made no comment, and not until the outer door had banged did Mike speak. 'I didn't get him full,' he said.

'Who did then? He's been with you, hasn't he?' Lizzie's voice conveyed neither displeasure nor amusement.

'Yes, he was along of me; I couldn't shake him off. It was at his suggestion we had a pint together ... And then—' Suddenly Mike's voice broke, and his head went up and back, and his rocketing laugh filled the room. He took out his handkerchief and dabbed his eyes and said between gasps, 'Me. I had to put the brake on because of him. Can you see me putting the brake on because of Harry Flannagan? I kept saying, "No. I'll just have a gill. . . . No, no," I said, "I never touch whisky." And there he was with a double and a pint at his elbow. I tell you I had to get him out while he was still on his legs. If I'd waited any longer I'd have to've carried him back.' His laughter eased to a gentle shaking, and he looked at Lizzie and said, quietly, 'It's funny, don't you think, me having to keep steady to look after him? He wouldn't leave me; I couldn't shake him off.'

It was funny; the anxiety, the worry, the pain, and her recrimination of him were once again washed away with his elusive endearingness, the unfair endearingness that had the power to blot out all but the feelings of the moment. With one accord they moved swiftly to each other, and his laughter rolling out again, he caught her up and swung her about.

Mary Ann's laughter joined his, but it was a little too loud and a little too high to be natural, and it was too full of relief to stay as laughter. This was the first time since her da had won that money that she had seen him and her ma laughing together and with their arms about each other. It meant that everything was going to be all right, no matter what her grannie did or how nice Mr. Quinton was.

Her laughter broke on a cry, and she fled from the room and through the kitchen into the scullery, and she leant her head on the sink and sobbed. But almost immediately she felt herself lifted up, and hiding her face, she buried it in her father's neck. And when Lizzie, stroking her head, said, 'Come, come, now we're going to see the bonfires,' her crying mounted, for it was the only way in which she could express her happiness at this moment.

CHAPTER SIX

SUNDAY

THE world was a beautiful place; there had never been any rain, or dullness, or darkness; there had never been any worry, fear or anxiety, for was not the sun shining brightly, and wasn't she walking in the country? In the country, mind, where the big trees grew, hand in hand with her da!

Not only was Mike solid and sober but he had on a new suit, and to crown his well-set-up appearance he was wearing on his head not the usual cap but a trilby. Mary Ann's gaze continually lifted from his face to the hat, and her heart was so swollen with pride that it was ready to burst from her body. Oh, he looked lovely in his new hat. Never, never in the world was there anybody who looked so wonderful as her da. Only one cloud touched him and the morning – Sarah Flannagan's eyes had not beheld the glory of him. Before they had left the house she had watched Sarah depart for Mass, and she had failed to induce her da to walk round by the church on their journey to the country in the hope that they would encounter Sarah coming out.

The thought of her enemy made Mary Ann once again put her hand tentatively towards the back of her head and feel the lump that even after a week had subsided very little. She touched it almost lovingly, for had she not received it in defence of her da?

On the morning following the events of Coronation Day Sarah had cornered her round the bottom of the back lane between the store shed of Tullis's outdoor beer shop and the Colyers' backyard wall. There in the narrow alley she had pinned her against the wall, and in language not strictly of school standard had accused Mike of making her da drunk and making her ma nearly throw a fit, and keeping them all up half the night, and, what was more, causing her da to lose the first shift in years because his head was so bad he couldn't raise it from the pillow.

Mary Ann had stoutly denied these accusations, saying that her da was solid and sober as everybody in the street knew, and he had never been inside a bar or smelt beer. As for Mr. Flannagan, he was a disgrace. Hadn't she seen him with her very own eyes being dragged into the house by Mrs. Flannagan? That was when her da was taking them all to see the bonfires. And hadn't Mr. Flannagan made a show of himself by fighting Mrs. Flannagan because he wanted to go along with her da?

That Sarah's rage only led her to bang Mary Ann's head repeatedly against the wall said something for her control. Whether she would have continued this restrained retaliation until she had accomplished Mary Ann's entire insensibility cannot be known, for Mary Ann's cries brought Mrs. Colyer from her house, and Sarah reluctantly departed at a run.

The attitude of her parents concerning this attack was not quite clear to Mary Ann; even her da gave her little sympathy, and her ma did not show the slightest sign of going to Mrs. Flannagan and telling her off. There was, she felt, injustice somewhere; but to explain it, even to herself, was beyond her. Only one thing was sure in her mind concerning the affair, she had got this great bump on her head and nearly died in defence of her da.

'That's the farm,' said Mike.

'Oh.'

Mary Ann looked over the yellow-green fields towards the

flat-faced red-brick house and asked, 'Will the cottage be that size?'

'No. No, of course not,' said Mike. 'You know the size of cottages; they're like the little houses at the Quay Corner, two or three rooms at the most. But there's bound to be a good patch of garden.'

'And how'll I get to school?'

'You'll have to take the bus. But wait, I haven't got it yet.'

The altered tone of her father's voice made her lift her eyes searchingly up to him. His smile had gone and there was a stiff straightness about his face that brought the shadow of anxiety back for a moment to dim the sun, and caused her to resort to praying rapidly that the job might be his.

There was no one in the farmyard except a sow with its stomach almost trailing the ground, and the sight of it brought Mary Ann from an anxious conversation with the Holy Family. She had never seen such a fat pig. She stared at it amazed, fascinated by the wobbling enormity of its flesh.

Mike left her to her wonderment and went towards a brick cowshed standing stark in its newness from amongst the time-worn, rather tumble-down buildings of the yard.

'Mr. Campbell?' He spoke to a man who was unscrewing a nozzle from a pipe, and the man turned his head and said peremptorily, 'Yes, I'm Campbell. What is it?'

The tone slightly nonplussed Mike. But he went forward, and in a carefully guarded voice, said, 'I've come about the job; I was told you wanted a hand.'

'Oh, that.' Mr. Campbell straightened his back, his eyes still directed towards the nozzle. 'You're too late, that's been filled nearly a week.'

The expression on Mike's face did not change, but he stood staring down at the bowed head of this under-sized little man and making a great effort to check a swift rush of temper. He hadn't got the job. That was bad, but by now he was, in a way, inured to disappointment; it was the offhandedness of the man that angered him. He was still intent on the pipe; it was as if he were alone, that nothing existed for him but the nozzle of the artificial milker.

Abruptly Mike turned and walked away, out of the cowshed, across the yard towards the road again, holding out his hand silently to Mary Ann as he went. His return was so quick and unexpected that she had to drag her thoughts back from the fascinating ugliness of the pig to take in exactly what this quick departure meant.

She moved towards him and put her hand in his. And so swift was his stride that she had to run to keep abreast of him. She could see he was flaming mad – she used his own expression to describe his temper – and she was sensible enough not to anger him further by asking senseless questions.

They had gone some way down the road when they were both halted by a shout. 'Hi! Hi, there!'

Mike turned slowly, paused a moment, then walked back towards the farmer. They stopped within a few yards of each other, and there was no prelude in the farmer's speech. 'Old Lord will be needing men; he's bought Coffin's farm. . . . You know Lord's place?'

Mike nodded.

'It was only sold yesterday. Coffin's taking his men with him. There'll be two empty cottages. . . . I suppose you want a cottage?'

'Yes.'

'Well, I would try there.' Then as if to explain his previous disinterest he added before turning away, 'I'm having trouble with the new machine. Not used to it yet.'

He had almost reached his farm-gate when Mike shouted, 'Thank you, sir.'

The man raised his hand in acknowledgment, and Mike and Mary Ann went on their way again.

'Are we going to Mr. Lord's, Da?'

'No.'

'What for not?'

'Because it would be no use.'

'Why?'

'Oh.' Mike moved his head impatiently.

'If there's a cottage, Da?'

'You know who Mr. Lord is, don't you?'

At the moment Mary Ann didn't know; she had to delve back in her mind. . . . Mr. Lord? . . . Mr. Lord? . . . 'Oh yes.' She smiled. 'He's the man with the big stone walls round his house, with the big trees inside. You can't see the house. It's up beyond the cemetery.'

Mike nodded.

'And he's got a wood farther along with barbed wire round and you can't get in.'

Mike nodded again.

But Mary Ann could see no reason why this should keep them from visiting Mr. Lord. Her mind groped to understand all her da had left unsaid. Then suddenly she understood. Mr. Lord was . . . the Lord. It was the nickname the men gave him in the yard, and her da had once worked in Lord's yard. And he had left when he was having a lot of talk about his theories. . . . Mr. Lord and the Lord were the same person. Her spirits sank to a still lower ebb, and any hope of the cottage sank with them.

They boarded a bus that took them into Hebburn and then on to Jarrow, and when they alighted at the Ben Lomond, Mike said, 'You run off home, I won't be long.' And after one long look at him, Mary Ann turned silently away. The sun had gone, the day was dull, almost dark again.

She walked through the empty streets. The shops were

shut and there was no one even sitting on a step, because it was Sunday. Everywhere looked bare and deserted and the atmosphere touched her low spirits and sent her off at a run to seek the security of the kitchen and the comfort of her mother. But her running ceased abruptly when she entered her street, for there she saw small groups gathered together on the pavement. There must, she surmised, have been a row. But not on a Sunday, surely. You could have rows up to quite late on a Saturday night, and they'd be quite in order, but it was shocking to have them on a Sunday. Smugly the thought came to her that it couldn't be her family, anyway. No, but it was in Mulhattans' Hall where the row was. She had evidence of this as she neared her home, and her surprise was almost stupefying as she mounted the stairs, for the shouting was coming right from the top of the house, and it was Mrs. McBride who was doing it.

She passed Miss Harper's open door, and also the Quigleys', and when she reached her own landing Mrs. McBride was shouting at her mother, 'Why didn't you tell me, you could have tipped me the wink?'

She stood in the doorway watching them. Mrs. McBride was all dressed up in her Mass clothes, the tight black coat and the black felt hat she wore only on Sundays. Her mother was wearing the big apron she put round her when she was doing the dinner; she had the oven cloth in one hand and she kept pulling it through the other; but she didn't answer Mrs. McBride; and Fanny cried 'The whole place has known except me, and never a thing would I have heard yet but for something Mary Prout said at the church door. She was talking to May Brice. "Join the army and see the world," she said, "and join the Salvation Army and see the other world. Wait till old Fan gets wind of it, Jack'll wonder which cuddy's kicked him." It wasn't long afore I had it out of her, and I nearly died when I heard. And let her take what she got, for I wouldn't believe a word of it. Yet there's no smoke without fire, and I came tearing home and tackled him, and he admitted it.'

She became silent for a moment, and her gaze turned inwards. She was seeing the astonishment on her son's face and feeling the tearing hurt of his words. 'Yes, it's Joyce Scallen. And I'm going to marry her. And just you try and stop me. And you make that rowdy tongue of yours go about it and I'll do it right away, I won't wait.'

But her tongue was her only weapon, the only weapon she knew of, and she had lashed it at him, and not only at him but at the whole family of Scallens.

Lizzie said gently, 'It might turn out all right. Just give them a chance.'

'A chance! A chance to do what, I ask you? Lead a hell of a life? What chance is there for happiness between a Hallelujah and a Catholic . . . because she won't turn? Do you know what her old father said to me? "It must be the will of God," he said. And he said that God was showing Jack the way and he'd be saved yet.'

'You see,' said Lizzie, 'Mr. Scallen's taking it quietly. There'd be more chance with Jack if you could take it quietly an' all; you'd best Mr. Scallen at his own game then.'

'So you think like me,' cried Fanny, 'he means something? Perhaps he's known about it all along, although the old swine said he hadn't.' She flung her short arms wide apart and lifted her eyes to the ceiling. 'Oh, what am I to do? Before you know it there'll be our Jack leading the band and knocking bloody hell out of the big drum, and I'll never be able to raise me head again on the whole Tyneside.'

Try as she might Lizzie could not suppress a smile, but her concern for the old woman was genuine, so much so that she addressed her by her Christian name as she said, 'Don't worry, Fanny, he'll not do anything silly; he's a sensible lad, is Jack; only be patient with him.'

'Patient!' Fanny spoke quietly now. She looked suddenly deflated. 'I've always been patient with him. Now if our Phil had done this I could have understood it. But not Jack. Not him.' Shaking her head, she moved towards the door, saying, 'This is what comes of missing Mass and neglecting his duties. It's two years since he was at them.' She paused near Mary Ann, and in a broken voice, said, 'There's worse things than drink, hinny. Remember that.' She patted her on the head, then went slowly down the stairs.

Mary Ann watched her. There was a lump the size of an egg in her throat – Mrs. McBride was crying.

Her mother was standing by the table waiting for her to speak, but she couldn't for the moment, and Lizzie said, 'He didn't get it?'

She shook her head.

'Where is he?'

'At the Ben Lomond. He won't be long.'

Lizzie turned away and Mary Ann said, 'The farmer was nice. ... He was sorry and he told me da about another job.'

'Where?' Lizzie turned about again.

'At Mr. Lord's.'

'Lord's?'

'Yes. Beyond the cemetery.'

'The shipyard man?'

'Yes. Me da said it was no use going.'

'He was right.'

Mary Ann watched her mother go into the scullery. She too looked deflated. There was no comfort or security even here; and the whole world must be sad when Mrs. McBride was crying.

CHAPTER SEVEN

THE LAST STRAW

ALTHOUGH during the following week Mike was never paralytic, his inability to reach this stage being, he himself confessed, merely owing to the weakness of the beer, he was at times well set. Yet he had made no oration in the street, and hadn't sung until he reached the stairs. And although on this particular night he had to be alternately pulled and coaxed away from Miss Harper's fast-closed door, where he insisted on serenading her, not untunefully, with 'He was her man, but he did her wrong', this had been the only incident of the week.

But this incident, which had amused everyone in the house with the exception of Miss Harper and the Shaughnessys themselves, was the means of snapping the taut thread of Michael's strained nerves. He had sat for the examination, and during the waiting period prior to the results being made known, he was up in the clouds and down in the depths ten times a day ... yes, he would be telling Lizzie, he felt he had answered most of the questions correctly; or no, he was sure he hadn't and had mugged everything.

It was earlier in the evening of Mike's serenading that Michael's pal had dashed in to say his parents had received a letter saying he had passed for the Grammar School. The last post of the day had been to Mulhattans' Hall and Michael had done his best to be pleased for his pal, but even his best was a poor effort, and Lizzie, keen disappointment filling her together with a heart torn with pity for her son, tried to reassure him that there was still tomorrow and that they wouldn't send all the notices out together. Michael had made no response to this except to shrug her hand off his shoulder and go into the other room and close the door after him.

It was eleven o'clock the same night, when Lizzie had to arouse Mary Ann from her bed to go down and coax Mike from Miss Harper's door, that Michael had begun to cry. His crying at first had been the broken sobs of a child, but when his father staggered into the room his sobs turned to angry gasps and when Mike, still singing, flopped into a chair he sat up and screamed at him: 'Shut up, you drunken pig you! I hate you, you rotten drunken pig!'

There followed a short surprised silence, which was suddenly broken by Michael crying again, 'Damn! damn! damn!' He thumped the bedclothes with his fist, and when Lizzie rushing to the bed tried to draw him to her he sprang up, thrusting her aside, and ran to where Mike, silent now, was surveying him. 'I wish you were dead, do you hear?' He pushed his face towards his father, who was now wearing a fuddled, surprised expression. 'They wouldn't let me pass because they knew about you ... everybody knows about you. I wish you'd fall from the top of a mast and be smashed to bits.'

'Michael!' Lizzie dragged at him, but with the strength of his passion he again thrust her off, crying at her now, 'Why don't you go away and leave him? Why do you make us stay here? I won't stay; I'll go to me grannie's.'

With the aid of the chair Mike rose. He seemed much steadier than when he had sat down and his voice was only slightly fuddled when he said, 'Be quiet, do you hear?'

'I won't! I won't! I loathe you. I wish you were ...'

'Quiet!' The shout vibrated from the walls, and in the

92

silence that followed they all stood still, seeming to be stunned by the force of the order.

Mike was staring down into his son's face and his expression was frightening, but it seemed powerless wholly to intimidate Michael, who continued to glare up at him, and after a moment Mike turned from the loathing in the boy's eyes and, with only a slight sway in his walk, went towards the room.

Mary Ann watched her mother lead Michael to the bed. She watched her tenderly cover him up, then lie down on top of the bed beside him, and not until she began to shiver did she go to the corner where her bed was, and, climbing in, turn her face to the wall and thrust her fingers into her ears to shut out the sound of Michael's crying.

It was a long time later when her mother came and stood over her. She did not let her know she was awake, but kept her eyes closed. She heard her walk softly away and turn the light out, and when the darkness fell on her lids she opened her eyes and stared into the blackness. She felt her mother move across the room and into the bedroom. The door clicked softly. Then there was no sound. She could not even hear Michael's breathing. Poor Michael. Her thoughts were tender towards him. If only he had passed the exam, then he might not have minded about her da so much.

The words Michael had used to her father had not shocked her, for he had expressed them many times to her, and whereas she had always fought him when he upbraided Mike, tonight for the first time she felt in sympathy with him. But this did not mean she was less sorry for her father or that she condemned him, it only meant that within her small body was the capacity for understanding the agony of the personal disappointments of childhood.

For what seemed to her hours and hours she lay on her back staring into the darkness. Once a car passed down the street, and once Miss Harper had a fit of coughing and it sounded as if she was in the room. She was slowly falling into sleep when she was recalled to her wakefulness by the fog-horn wailing up the river, and she felt a little guilty that she should sleep when there was all this trouble in the house. Hastily she determined that she must keep awake. This was her last thought before sleep overtook her, but then it was a troubled sleep, for her dreams were on the surface and once or twice as was usual with her she told herself she was dreaming. Once she imagined she heard Michael get out of bed and go into the scullery, the door of which was near the foot of her bed, but it was all mixed up in her dreams.

She was not sure what woke her; perhaps it was the smell – she had been dreaming that she was being choked by the smell. She tried to sit up but found that her head was heavy and that she felt very sleepy. She also felt a little sick. Now why should she be feeling sick, for she had eaten no supper and she hadn't eaten any sweets for two days? It was a gassy smell, like when her mother turned the tap on and dropped the match and the gas came out of the oven and filled the scullery.

She was never to know exactly what drove her to rise against all her opposing inclinations and stagger to Michael's bed. It was empty, but she knew where he was . . . he was in the scullery. The scullery door was closed, and when she pushed it open the gas met her in a sickening wave. She could not see Michael but she knew he was there.

Staggering in her run, she burst into the bedroom and having groped her way to the bed pulled madly at her mother.

'What is it?' Lizzie was sitting up. 'My God!' Almost immediately she got the smell of the gas and was out of bed.

'Michael.'

'He's in the scullery.' Mary Ann's words were cut short by being knocked on her bottom in Lizzie's dive for the door.

'Wha's up? Wha's the row?' Mike's voice, thick with sleep,

came from the bed, and Mary Ann, scrambling to him, shook him by his slack hanging arm, crying, 'It's Michael – he's in the scullery and the gas is on.'

Again she was almost knocked flat, and by the time she reached the door she heard her father's voice coming from the other side of the kitchen, saying, 'God in Heaven, what's he done?'

It was many hours later that Mary Ann recollected they were the only words she heard her da speak that night. It was her ma who did the talking. Fiercely she whispered, 'Open the window, and the scullery one, too, and let a draught through . . . and do it quietly.'

As Mike swiftly obeyed her command she said to Mary Ann, 'Get me the torch from the cupboard – mind the table.'

Mary Ann groped her way to the cupboard, groped for the torch, then groped her way back to where her mother was kneeling on the floor. Lizzie snatched the torch from her fingers and, switching it on, plunged its light on to Michael's face.

Mary Ann stared down at her brother. His face looked pink and smooth and swollen. He looked sound asleep, very sound asleep. She watched her mother grab him by the shoulders and shake him. She allowed her eyes to travel to her father's legs and up to where they disappeared beneath his shirt-tail, but she could not lift them to his face . . . until he bent his body over his son and his face came into the beam of the torch, and then she saw it was grey, an awful whitish grey, and that his eyes, although sunk deep into his head, had, at the same time, a popping look. His whole appearance looked wild and not a little fantastic. His strong wiry hair was standing up from his head in points and his shirt seemed too short and tight for his body.

Mary Ann moved swiftly back as he hauled Michael from the floor and carried him to the window. Her mother followed, directing the light towards the floor. Mary Ann looked to where her father, silhouetted against the darkness of the night and the blackness of the houses opposite, was shaking Michael, and when after a moment Michael's head lolled against his shoulder Lizzie turned to Mary Ann gasping, 'Get your things on, quick.' And she followed her to the bed saying, 'Run for the doctor, the nearest – that one off Ormond Road – Pimsel.' Her talking was in staccato whispers. 'Tell him ... tell him that Michael ... wait.' She stopped, and Mary Ann saw her turn to the window. 'No, don't go yet. Look, run down to Mrs. McBride's. Go quietly without your shoes. Let yourself out the back door. She sleeps with the window open a bit. Try not to raise the house. Ask her to come. Go on now.' She pushed Mary Ann to the door, putting a coat about her petticoat and her thin bare arms as she went.

Mary Ann did not need to be told to hurry or to make no noise. She was used to the stairs in the dark, and when her swift light tread made them creak she took no notice for she knew they always creaked at night – it was the souls in purgatory being made to use them as a tread-mill that caused the creaking.

The cold of the yard struck up through her stockinged feet as she closed the back hall door softly after her and she knew a moment of fear at finding herself in the backyard made unfamiliar with the night. When she reached Mrs. McBride's bedroom window she raised herself to the sill by digging her toes into the wall, and she called softly through the narrow opening, 'Mrs. McBride.' On her third call she heard a rustling and she knew that she had woken the old woman, but not until she had repeated the call did she hear her speak.

'Holy Mother of God,' said Mrs. McBride; and Mary Ann said, 'It's me, Mrs. McBride ... Mary Ann.'

There was a pause before Mrs. McBride answered,

'Mary Ann Shaughnessy? In the name of God, what's up?'

'Sh!' said Mary Ann. 'Listen. Me ma sent me for you . . . our Michael's bad.'

'Bad?'

'Yes.'

Mrs. McBride didn't seem to be unduly disturbed by this and Mary Ann had to say the dreaded words, 'He's put his head in the gas oven.'

It seemed to Mary Ann that almost in a single blinking of her eyelids Mrs. McBride was at the back door. Dragging a coat over her dirty nightdress with one hand, she pulled Mary Ann into the scullery with the other and pushed her ahead into the room and across it; then quietly unbolting her door she drew Mary Ann into the hallway and preceded her up the stairs. She did all this, to Mary Ann's amazement, with the quietness and swiftness of a cat.

From the moment Mrs. McBride entered the room she took command of the situation. She bent over Michael where he was now lying on the bed and put her hand inside his pyjama jacket for a moment, then turning to Mike, she said, 'Hoist him up and get him walking, he's not gone. . . . That's it.' She got on one side of him. 'Come on now, keep him going. Make up a good dose of hot salt water, Lizzie.' She turned her head in Lizzie's direction without pausing in her walk. 'He'll come to. That's it, keep him at it Mike, it's air he wants.'

In the light of the torch Mary Ann stood watching her da and Mrs. McBride dragging Michael back and forward between the window and the bed, his feet trailing like dead things. It was a strange and weird trio, made more fantastic still by the torchlight. Suddenly Michael's body stiffened, his head came up and his chest swelled out and he retched and was sick over the floor.

'That's the ticket, get it up, lad. He won't need the salt-water now.' When they got him back to the bed again and

97

Lizzie held a dish under his head, Mrs. McBride exclaimed in much the same tone as another would use when viewing an objet d'art, 'Lovely . . . beautiful.'

Mary Ann moved a little closer. Michael was lying gasping now, his head moving heavily from side to side, and she could have thrown herself into Mrs. McBride's arms when she heard her say, 'He'll be as right as rain; there's no need to worry.'

'Could I light the gas now?' asked Lizzie.

'Ay, of course, it'll all be gone by now. But I'd pull down the blinds,' said Fanny, 'or Nancy Cooper'll have her two bleary eyes glued to her window . . . she never sleeps.'

It was not until the gas was lit that Mary Ann saw her father clearly. He didn't seem like her da at all . . . his face seemed altered completely. It looked to her as if something had sucked all the blood from it, and his eyes looked – she could not allow herself even to think how his eyes looked, for fear was the last thing she would associate with her da.

It wasn't until Mike dragged his eyes from his son's face to gaze from one to the other of them in stupefied perplexity that he became conscious of his state of undress. He turned from the bed and went slowly into the room, and Lizzie, bending over the boy, called softly, 'Michael, Michael.' For answer he rolled his head and retched again, and Fanny, straightening her back with an effort, said, 'Ah, he'll do fine. There's nothing to worry about. You should have seen my Florrie the night she did it, when she found young Bob Lancaster had given her a bellyful. It was nearly touch and go that night and many's the time I've wondered since if it wouldn't have been better to let her go, for there she is now with seven round her, and to a no-good waster like Fred Boyle, and her young Bob gone off God knows where, and him the only one she gives a hoot for. Life's crazy, I've said it afore, but thank God even at the longest it's short. And it can't be short enough for me.' She sighed heavily, and Mary

Ann knew she was thinking of Jack who was really going to marry Joyce Scallen. But what was that to worry about compared with what had nearly happened.

She shivered, and Mrs. McBride turned to her, saying, 'What, are you cold, hinny? Why don't you jump into bed?' She bent over her, her breasts pressing out the front of her coat like great inflated balloons. And Mary Ann wanted to lay her head between them and put her arms about the not too clean neck and cry with relief, for had she not saved their Michael and was she not as anxious as her ma to keep the disgrace from the neighbours, for Mary Ann was fully aware of the disgrace that clung to a family should one of them stick their head in the gas oven. You were put in the papers then and everybody knew about you. That was why her mother had stopped her going for the doctor, for if the doctor had come it would have been all over the place and her da would have got all the blame. She glanced towards the bedroom door and Mrs. McBride said, 'Don't worry, hinny, he'll be all right an' all, he's only getting into his things. Jump into bed with you now.'

Slowly she did as she was told and when Fanny's lips came down to hers she did not offer her cheek but returned the old woman's kiss. She watched her go and bend over Michael again, then walk towards the door pulling her coat about her. She saw her ma follow and she could hear them talking but not what they said. She saw Mrs. McBride patting her mother, then she went out and her mother closed the door softly after her and returned to Michael.

It was some little time before her father came out of the room. He did not go to the bed but stood looking towards it to where Lizzie knelt stroking the boy's head. Michael was recovered sufficiently to cry again, but softly, and after a time, during which Lizzie gave no heed to Mike's presence, he went back into the room. Mary Ann watched her mother make a drink for Michael, she watched him refuse it and then be coaxed to drink it, then she saw Lizzie lie on top of the bed and put her arms about him, and she felt nothing but pity, until once again her father entered the kitchen. And when he stood silently looking at his wife and son the pity for Michael and sorrow for her mother combined into a fear, and the fear was formed around their allegiance and what it would mean to her da.

When once again her father returned to the room she saw her mother gently disengage herself from Michael and follow him. She had not turned out the light, so that meant she was coming back. Mary Ann sat swiftly up in bed and pressed her ears in the direction of the bedroom but the only sound she could hear was of a low murmur, and it was of her mother's voice. Her ears were so attuned to listening that she could distinguish what emotion was present in the murmuring of her parents' speech, but even without this facility she would have recognized disaster from the low, dead murmur of her mother's voice.

Knowing that she might be caught in the act did not prevent her from getting out of bed and moving swiftly towards the door. She had no need to bend down to the keyhole, for the door was ajar. She stood at the side nearest the opening, close to the wall, and listened to her mother. At first she could not disentangle the quick, low speech, but then she began to make out the words. They were dead words, yet alive with dread significance. They came to Mary Ann, bearing all the sorrow in the world. 'Don't think this silent, remorseful attitude of yours will touch me. You've tried everything in the past. You found talking yourself silly didn't work; well, you can save yourself this effort for it won't work either. If he had died I would have killed you, do you hear? Oh how I loathe you, you great weak hulk. ... Well, it's finished, finally finished. I'm going.'

In the awful silence that followed, into which Mike threw

no plea, Mary Ann stumbled back to bed; whatever more there was to be said could not surpass this. She lay watching the door. Her breathing seemed to have ceased, until suddenly, her lungs demanding air, she drew into her narrow chest deep gulps that almost choked her.

Lizzie came out of the room and stood for a moment, her hand pressed to her throat, before slowly moving towards the light and turning it down to a mere glimmer. After the springs of Michael's bed creaked, there was no more sound.

Mary Ann lay for a long time trying to discern objects through the glimmer, trying to shut out the thoughts that conjured up the future without her da, trying to stave off the dawn. Yet when its first light showed on the paper blind she realized she must have fallen asleep, for the gas was out and she hadn't seen her mother get up and turn it off. Soon she knew her da would come out of the room and get ready for work, and he would leave the house, and perhaps before he returned her mother would have taken them away to their grannie's. This might be the last time she would see him leave for work. The thought brought her from the bed. She must say something to him, tell him she would always love him and when she grew up she would look after him.

Gently she pushed the open door wider, and her eyes peered towards the bed. But he wasn't in it, he was sitting on the box to the side of the window. She could see the great dark huddled shape of him, and she was about to move softly forward when her step was checked by a sound coming from him. It was a familiar enough sound when connected with herself or Michael, or her mother, or anyone else in the world, but not with her da. It filled her body with a great, deep, unbearable pity. She stood listening to the sound until she could stand it no longer. It did not drive her to him to spread her comfort over him but back to her bed to lie huddled and sobbing herself. A god had fallen, not through his sins but through his weakness – for gods did not cry.

By the nine o'clock post the letter had arrived to say that Michael had passed for the Grammar School, but it did not make much difference; it had come too late.

CHAPTER EIGHT

SOME CALL IT AUTO-SUGGESTION
(IT'S THEIR IGNORANCE, GOD HELP THEM)

As Father Owen listened to the child his heart grew heavy, not only with the weight of her sorrow but with the sorrow that seemed to be the heritage of all such as Mary Ann. Their very joy was tinged with sorrow, made so by their sensitiveness, a quality which should have been used merely to appreciate the finer things of life but which was deformed by constant worry. As he listened to her voice relating the happening of the last few days his mind rebelled against the sentence inflicted on childhood, a sentence inflicted by the parents themselves. Life at this stage should be a joyous thing; God made it so; away with all the twaddle that it was He who sent suffering.

Mary Ann was saying, 'He doesn't talk, Father . . . he says nothing, and he hasn't been full. He went out last night but he came back solid and sober.'

'When is your mother going?'

'Saturday, Father, I think.'

'And you're not going to your grandmother's?'

'No. She said only last night she'd got a furnished room round Hope Street and we go in on Saturday, and she's got the promise of a job, and Michael and me are to have our dinner at school.'

'And your da says nothing?'

'No, nothing; and he wouldn't let me pour the water over his head when he washed.'

'And does he seem upset at your mother going?'

Mary Ann did not answer the priest for the moment – upset could not describe the state her da was in, he seemed gone away somehow, dead. She was no consolation to him, and she knew, without knowing how she had come to the knowledge, that without her mother she had no power of her own to hold him. She herself could have done without even her mother as long as she had him, but in him it was her ma that infused the power to live. So she answered, 'When me ma goes I don't know what he'll do. I'm frightened, Father.'

'Now there's no need to be frightened. Just trust in God and everything will come out all right. For your penance, say one Our Father and one Hail Mary . . . make a good act of contrition.'

Slowly Mary Ann said the set piece – it was as if she were loath to leave the confessional and the comfort of the priest – she spread it out and was only induced to finish when Father Owen said, 'Now, good night, my child, and trust in God.'

'Good night, Father.'

When she left the box the priest, after a murmured prayer, followed her. There would be no other children after Mary Ann. He was so used to her manoeuvres that he almost judged the time by her now. He saw her light a candle, then kneel with uplifted face to the altar of the Holy Family, and he turned to the church door and went through the porch and stood on a step, drawing in the fresh air as he looked up and down the street.

It was quiet now, the traffic of the day having eased. The shops on the other side were closed, their doors locked and barred, all except the door leading to the office of Mayland's, the solicitor. Likely, Father Owen surmised, there was a meeting going on up in the Board Room there. Ah, he shook his head at himself, he wished he had just the smell of the money that had changed hands in that room today. .... But what was he thinking about? There would be no board meeting at this time of the evening. It was now six o'clock. Didn't his stomach tell him so? And what was more there were no cars about except one, and if he was not mistaken it was old Lord's. Likely it was him up there alone, settling the business of more land. What did he hope to do with it all? One thing was sure, he couldn't take it with him. Oh dear, dear; what men strove for. He shook his head again, this time at Mr. Lord.

Peter Lord was an old man now, and what was in his life? Money and land. Yet God help him, he wasn't to blame entirely. Thirty years ago he had been a man splendid in his prime and if he had only managed his private affairs with the same sagacity as he did his business he would undoubtedly have had an exceptionally happy life, but like many another able man before him he had to go and pick on a feather-brained vain piece of a girl, and what a life she had led him. And she had given him nothing, not even a child; and then to leave him when she thought he was going broke. Oh, she had been a right bad piece that. And there he was alone in that barracks of a house where he lived like a hermit. Life was strange. Just imagine, if he had had someone to pour out love on him as did that child back in the church there on that hot-headed devil of a father of hers, it would have made all the difference in the world.

'Oh, there you are, Mary Ann.' He stood to one side and made room for her on the step beside him in the half-open doorway. 'Have you been to confession?'

He was well aware, perhaps not that he was blind in the confessional, but that he was to Mary Ann an entirely different being when once out of the box, and of being quite incapable of recognizing her as the same child who a few minutes before had poured her heart out to him.

'Yes, Father,' said Mary Ann, but there was no smile on her face tonight as she said it.

'That's a good girl ... you'll be qualifying to lead the procession again next year, I can see that.'

'Yes, Father.' She managed a very faint smile. As he patted her head the sound of a car starting up made him turn his gaze up the street and as he watched it approach his hand became still on her head; then swiftly, without looking at her again, he gave her a little push backwards, saying, 'Stay there now.' And as Mary Ann stood within the shelter of the porch he stepped briskly to the kerb and hailed the driver of the car.

'Have you a minute?'

The car had not gathered any speed and Mr. Lord brought it to a standstill, saying, 'Hallo – what are you after now?'

'Have you a minute?'

'Yes, and nothing else, and even that is valuable.'

The priest laughed and was in no way put out at the brusqueness of the tone. 'Oh yes, yes. Don't I know.' He bent his face down to the open window and cast his eyes sidelong at the erect forbidding figure sitting behind the wheel. 'Well it's only two minutes of your time I want, and I'll pay you when my ship comes in, or perhaps I'll just leave it to God and good neighbours.'

'What are you after now?'

'What makes you think I'm after anything?'

'If I know you it's something to do with money.'

'You're wrong then, this time at any rate. But if you've got any going ...'

'Not a penny. Three hundred you had out of me last year.'

'Was it that much? Good gracious.'

'Was it that much!'

'Well, well, doesn't it mount up?'

Mr. Lord surveyed the priest with a hard, forbidding look which did not intimidate Father Owen, who, putting his head and shoulders farther into the car, changed his tone and said, 'You can do me a favour if you would.'

There was no Yes or Nay or What is it? from Mr. Lord, but in still silence he waited for the priest to go on.

'I heard you'd bought up Coffin's farm.'

Still silence surrounded Mr. Lord.

'And I've heard,' said Father Owen, 'that Coffin took his hands with him, at least that's what I'm given to understand. They must have been fine workers; when a man gets good farm-hands these days he keeps them. Of course Coffin was good to the men. Didn't he have those two fine cottages built for them?'

Mr. Lord closed his blue-veined eyelids for a second, then stared ahead through the windscreen and said, 'Come to the point, I want to get home.'

'All right – I want you to give a man I know a job – it may be the making of him. Have you stocked up? Have you got your men?'

'No.' Mr. Lord turned his head slowly towards the priest. 'And I'm not stocking up with any of your riff-raff. I've had experience of your recommendations before and whoever you're wanting to palm off on me now would likely not be able to recognize one end of a cow from the other.'

'Ah, but you're wrong there – he's a right fine man with cows.'

Whether intentionally or otherwise Father Owen had adopted Mary Ann's voice and her words, and he had to laugh at himself for so doing. But his hilarity had an irritating effect on Mr. Lord. He moved his hand on the wheel saying, 'You're wasting your time.'

'Look, just a minute.' Father Owen stretched out his hand

and laid it gently on Mr. Lord's arm. 'If you were to give this man a chance it would likely mean the saving of a family.'

'Why should that particular point be any concern of mine?'

The two old men stared at each other. Then Father Owen brought back the dim past when this man and he had been firm friends before the bitterness of life had erected the barrier between Peter Lord and all men, by saying, 'Peter, do this one thing for me.'

The use of his Christian name seemed to have little or no effect upon Mr. Lord's feelings, for his countenance remained forbidding, but after a moment during which he seemed about to drive off despite the fact that Father Owen was half in and half out of the car, he asked, 'Who is it, and why are you so bent on getting him on a farm?'

Father Owen kept all eagerness from his voice as he said, 'Because it's his natural work – he's like a fish out of water in the yards.'

'But there's plenty of farm work going, they're crying out for farm hands.'

'Yes, but they're not issuing cottages to go with them; and you know yourself there are no set hours for a good farmhand, and the farms are so few and far between here that a man would have to stay on the job and travel home at odd times, and this fellow can't stick that. He's tried it. He wants his family with him. He's the kind of fellow who . . .' He did not finish this and add, 'who falls to pieces without his wife,' but said: 'Well, he'd pay you a good dividend in labour if you could settle him and his family in a cottage.'

'What's his name?'

'Shaughnessy.'

Mr. Lord turned in his seat until he was square to the priest. 'Shaughnessy?' he asked heavily.

'Yes, that's him . . . a big red-headed chap.'

'Ha, ha!' It was supposed to be a laugh, but resulted in a dry splitting crack of a sound. 'You want me to take Mike Shaughnessy on? Why, if he was the last man on God's earth I wouldn't give him breathing space. Do you know what he did in my yard last year, or tried to do?'

The priest remained sadly silent.

'He would have had the men out – like that.' He snapped his fingers; and Father Owen said lamely, 'I hear he's a good worker.'

'A good worker! – he won't do a bat of overtime except with his tongue; besides which he's never sober. What do you take me for? Good-bye, Father.'

The farewell salutation was weighed with sarcasm and Father Owen withdrew himself from the car, which almost immediately shot forward and away.

As he turned towards the church again there was Mary Ann looking at him from the step, and he walked up to her, and they surveyed each other in silence.

How much had she heard? Her eyes were so full of strangled hope. He said, 'Mr. Lord has a job and a cottage going for a farm-hand. I thought I might get it for your da.'

She did not reply but continued to gaze up at him.

'He's not feeling too well tonight – he's in a bit of a bad mood – or perhaps I just didn't put the case properly.' He smiled gently down at her. 'Now you, Mary Ann, would likely have put his case much better – I mean your da's.' His voice trailed off and he became uneasy under the fixed pain of her eyes. 'Well, we must never give up hope. Keep on praying, Mary Ann; it's amazing the miracles the Holy Family perform. Just you ask them for advice. They never fail you. Now I must be off to my tea. Good night, my child.'

He moved hastily into the church and her eyes followed him, but she did not speak, not even to answer his farewell, and after a moment she too moved away, walking slowly in the direction of home.

* * *

The kitchen was empty when she arrived, but she knew that both her parents were in, for her da's black cap was hanging on the back of the door and the table had not been cleared and her mother never went out without first clearing the table. She was removing her coat and hat when their voices came to her from the bedroom. They sounded normal, quiet voices and her hands became still and hope sprang afresh into her being and overwhelmed her for a moment, until, moving farther into the room, her father's voice, like the backwash of a mighty wave, sucked it away again.

'I'll allow you so much. . . . But don't take my word for it, have it done legally; you'll be safe then. . . . When are you going?'

'Saturday.'

'To your mother's?'

'No – a place in Hope Street.'

'Are you taking the bits?'

'No, it's furnished.'

'Well, you may as well sell them because I won't be staying here. Can I . . . see the bairns sometime?'

There was a pause before Lizzie answered, 'Yes.'

To Mary Ann the voices sounded even and untroubled; they sounded the same as when they were discussing something that had appeared in the *Shields Gazette*. They sounded like that but they weren't like that; they were final voices, voices that had ceased to shout or yell or fight, or even plead; they were voices from which emotion had been drained; and they frightened Mary Ann more than any other voices could have done. She fled into the scullery and, covering her face with her hands and pressing herself into the corner of the wall between the sink and the cupboard, she began to pray.

CHAPTER NINE

THE LORD

THE steps were very wide, the widest she had even seen attached to any house, and the house was the biggest she had ever seen. When she had pulled herself below the barbed wire and into the wood she had been scared at the size of the trees, at the thickness of the undergrowth and of the dim, weird light, but when she had emerged from the wood and seen across the meadow the house looking gaunt and weary with a sort of stripped look in the early morning sunshine she had been more than scared. It had taken her quite a time to cross the meadow and get through the fence. She hadn't seen a gate and she had walked through the pathless tangled garden, and here she was, standing on the top step, her hand hovering towards the great knobbly door-bell, and she was, in truth, scared out of her wits.

She knew she had had the dream in the night and that the Holy Family had told her to come and see the Lord himself, but they, as far as she could see, hadn't come with her, and never in all her life had she known fear such as this. She tried to recall the courage she had felt in the night when she had talked with the Virgin. She had actually gone right up to Heaven and seen the Virgin busy with her task of making babies, and the Holy Mother had stopped her work and took her on her knee and had listened to all that she had to say, and then she had told her what she must do. And St. Joseph himself had set her to the gate. And then she had woken up full of courage. The courage had kept her awake until daylight. It had helped her to dress and get past her mother, who was asleep on a shake-down near the fireplace, and out of the door without awakening anyone.

She reached up a little farther and touched the bell, and of its own volition it seemed to come out of the wall for a surprising length, and the clatter it made would have raised the dead. She was still gasping with the shock of it when the door opened.

To say whose face showed the more surprise would be difficult. Mary Ann had expected to be confronted by ... the Lord; instead, before her stood a thin old man in a baggy old suit. His head was long and pointed and without hair, and his shoulders stooped as if he were carrying a weight upon them, but it was his face that surprised Mary Ann. If she had not been overcome with fright and worry she would have laughed at it. His mouth hung open and his nose twitched like a rabbit's and sent the wrinkles across his cheeks with each twitch.

But of the two, she was the first to find her voice, and even if at first the words wobbled round her mouth reluctant to come out she made the effort and stammered, 'P ... please I came to see the Lord.'

'What?' The old man's voice sounded cracked.

'The Lord – I've come to see ... the Lord. I want to t-talk to him, if you please.'

'How did you get in here?'

'Through the hedge – the gate was fastened.'

'Through the hedge?' The baggy suit appeared to swell with indignation. 'You got in through the hedge?'

'Yes, under the barbed wire.'

'Well, the quicker you get out the better it will be for you. Now away with you.'

He pointed a shaking finger over her head, but she did not move, and he said, 'Did you hear me?'

Slowly Mary Ann's mouth drew to a button which would have been a warning to anyone who knew her, and she answered with deceptive quietness, 'I'm not going till I see the Lord.'

'You're not what?' The bones seemed to rattle within the suit. 'We'll see about that.' His hand made as if to descend on her, and she rasped at him, 'You touch me and I'll bite a piece out of you.'

His hand remained threateningly over her, but it said much for her attitude that it didn't descend on her, but his voice rose to a shrill yet muffled cry as he exclaimed, 'Get out of this!'

'Not until I've seen the Lord.' As she spoke she placed herself in front of the stanchion, making it impossible for him to close the door.

'In the name of all . . .!' Her defence staggered him, and his pursed lips threw bubbles from his mouth. 'You would . . . defy me? Well, we'll see about that.'

'I'll scream, mind, if you touch me.' This threat seemed to intimidate him for a moment and he cast a backward glance over his shoulder; then whispered fiercely, 'You do if you dare.'

He made a grab at her but with a wriggle of her body she slipped past him and into the hall.

For a moment he stood looking at her as if she were something uncanny wafted into the morning from another world, and he asked, not without a trace of fear in his own voice, 'What are you after?'

'I want to see the Lord.'

'Who told you to come here?'

'The Holy Family.'

'The what—?'

'The Holy Family.'

Now understanding and a trace of compassion touched his face. The child was mad. But mad or no, he must get her

8 113

out of this before the master came down, so he said softly, 'The Holy Family sent you?'

'Yes.' Mary Ann nodded emphatically.

'Ah, well, yes, now I quite believe that. And what did they send you for?'

'To speak to the Lord.'

'What about?'

'About me da.'

'And what about your da?'

'I'm going to tell the Lord.'

'Now come, come.' He advanced slowly towards her. 'You tell me and I'll tell the mast . . . the Lord. How about that – eh?' As the old man came on Mary Ann backed away from him until she was at the foot of the stairs. Here she stopped and said, 'I won't tell nobody, only the Lord.'

'Now look here' – the old man's patience was swept away by the defiance that embodied this minute child – 'I'm having no more of it,' he declared. 'Do you hear? You get out of here this minute.'

'I'll scream mind . . . I will.' Mary Ann's warning cry had no effect this time and as his hand caught her none too gently by the shoulder she let out a high, shrill scream.

By now almost on the verge of hysteria himself, he was attempting to muffle her cries when a voice thundered over them. What it said neither of them knew but its mighty tone flung them apart and Mary Ann and the old man gazed up the staircase to where stood a figure with a pose of the avenging angel. Step by step the master of the house descended upon them, until he stood on the last step but one.

Had he, by one movement of his hand, now ordered them both to be shrivelled up in consuming flames it would not have been of the smallest surprise to Mary Ann. As he gazed down on her she actually stopped breathing, and when he thundered, 'What's this, may I ask?' she released her breath and opened her mouth still wider in an attempt to speak, but the old manservant forestalled her.

'I found her at the door, sir – she darted in.'

'What is she doing here?'

'She says she wants to see you.'

'Me?' Mr. Lord brought his eyes from Mary Ann and laid them on his servant, as if to extract without further preamble the meaning of the outrage.

'That's all I could get out of her, sir. I don't think she is' – he made an effort to straighten his bent shoulders as he delivered his verdict – 'compos mentis, sir. She says she was sent here by the Holy Family.'

Mr. Lord looked once more at Mary Ann, and Mary Ann made haste to press home the advantage she imagined the servant had unwittingly opened for her.

'He's right,' she said, in a voice that was a mere reflection of her normal and anything but quiet tone, 'They did, last night. Go to the Lord, they said, and tell him what a grand man your da is, and everything will come all right.'

Mr. Lord's bushy eyebrows gathered and hung over his cheek-bones like miniature palm trees.

At this point, collecting the shreds of her shattered courage, she half turned her back on the servant, and stretching to her fullest height, whispered confidentially in much the same tone as she used when addressing God, 'Lord, I want to talk to you.'

After staring down at her for a moment longer Mr. Lord made an impatient movement and he shook himself as if throwing off some benumbing spell. 'Not this morning, no time.' He thrust her aside as he descended the last stair and grimly, in an aside, said to the old servant, 'Get rid of her.'

Mary Ann heard. The new world that seemed almost within her grasp was dissolving before her eyes. She was in the actual presence of the Lord whose power equalled God's and to whom all things were possible. This man could give her da a job; he could give them a cottage, and in a cottage in the country they would be fast closed round and safeguarded from separation – if only her da could offer her ma a cottage in the country then she wouldn't leave him; she couldn't leave him if he'd give her a cottage in the country.

'Lord. Lord.' She dived at him and gripped his hand. 'If you only knew what a grand man me da is you'd give him the job.'

Mr. Lord's veined hand hung slackly between the two small hands that clawed at it. 'What job?' he asked quietly.

'On the farm – he's a grand man with horses and things – he knows all about. . . .'

'Who sent you here?' Mr. Lord released his hand slowly from hers.

'I told you Lord – The Holy Family.'

'Now, now' – the voice was grim – 'none of that. Father Owen sent you, didn't he?'

'He did not . . . Father Owen? No.'

'Don't lie. You were the child that was standing at the church door last night, weren't you, while we were talking?'

'I was standing there, but he didn't send me, and I couldn't hear all you said – I heard some, and I knew you had a job going that would have just suited me da and I went home and prayed to the Holy Family. . . .'

'Father Owen told you to do that?'

'Yes . . . no . . . No, I always pray to them on me own.'

'The scheming old rascal!' Mary Ann heard the muttered words and her own troubles were forgotten for the moment as she came to the defence of her beloved priest.

'He's not a rascal; he's a fine man, as fine as me da, and don't you say a word against him. And anyway you'll burn in Hell for daring to call a priest a rascal. Maggie Simmond's

Aunt Nellie spilled a big panful of boiling fat over herself and she died, and that was just after she'd had words with the priest, so there . . . look out.'

'Here, here, don't be cheeky. And come along. You've told enough lies and trash.'

The old servant once again bore down on Mary Ann, and this time she turned on him like a wild cat. 'I'm not telling lies, I'm telling the truth. After I had the dream I kept awake and I got up when the blind got a bit light on it and I come all this way to talk to the Lord about me da. And Father Owen's a lovely priest. D'you hear? And he put me in the May Procession, right at the head.' She seemed to be watching her voice as she sent it yelling up at the old bent figure. Then for a moment her face showed comical surprise as she heard it change. It began to wobble and crack, and her mouth began to quiver. She knew what was about to happen, and she fought against it with all her might, shouting even louder. 'There's a pair of you, so there is. You don't believe anything. You're like Sarah Flannagan, that's what you are. You wouldn't do much for God if the divil was dead.' And now, feeling that her case was hopeless and that her plea had failed, she turned on Mr. Lord, crying in deep earnest, 'You can keep your job and your old horses, and the cottage; me da'll get a job on a farm. They'll jump at him, for he's a fine, steady man – he can work like a black. And me ma'll go back to him when he gets a job with a cottage. You'll see. So there.' She nodded her head up at him in short, sharp nods; then turning blindly to what she thought was the front door, she stumbled into the dining-room.

The manservant, about to haul her out, was checked by Mr. Lord, who thrust his arm across the doorway, and after a moment of watching Mary Ann walking bewilderedly about the room, he said, 'Bring my breakfast.'

'But sir, she—'

'You heard what I said.'

One old man looked at the other. Then the servant who gave off his displeasure like the skunk does its smell, walked reluctantly away kitchenwards; and Mr. Lord went into the room and sat down at the table.

He did not look at Mary Ann who was standing now before the great empty fireplace staring down on to the dusty hearth, her back turned purposely to him, but he moved the crockery which was set on a none too clean cloth on the corner of the long massive dining table first one way and then another. Then abruptly he commanded, 'Come here!'

Mary Ann did not at once turn towards him; she sniffed a number of times and moved her shoulders. Thus having expressed her independence, she turned slowly about and walked to the table, her eyes cast down.

'Your name is Shaughnessy, isn't it?'

'Yes.' It was a very small voice.

'Does your father know you've come here?'

'Oh no. He said it was no use coming.'

'So he did know you were coming?'

'No. No; he didn't. He said that the Sunday we went to the farm up Pelaw way. The job was gone there, but the farmer told him about you.'

'And he said it was no use coming?'

'Yes.'

'How right he was.'

'Well, he doesn't want your job. You can keep. . . .'

'All right. All right.' He hastily lifted his hand to check her swiftly rising voice.

'He's a grand man.'

'Yes. Yes.'

'He is. He is.' Twice her chin was jerked up at him.

'Very well. . . . Ah, there you are.' It was with evident relief that he hailed the servant entering the room with a tray. And when the man, placing a dish before him, lifted the cover, the audible sniff from Mary Ann caused him to look at her with a swift searching glance.

She had been unable to prevent the sniff and she bowed her head in shame. She was hungry, but she'd rather starve to death than take even a bit of fried bread from the nasty old devil.

'Have you had any breakfast?'

'. . . No.' Her eyes, half raised, were just on a level with the big plate on which lay two pieces of fried bread, two rashers of bacon, an egg and two halves of a tomato.

'That'll do.' Mr. Lord, making to attack his breakfast, gave the curt order. But on this occasion, the old man was apparently deaf.

'Ben.'

'Yes, sir.'

'You heard me.'

Ben walked slowly to the door and passed into the hall, where Mr. Lord's voice, which nearly lifted Mary Ann from the ground, halted him.

'Ben!'

'Yes, sir?' Ben's disapproving body appeared in the door-way again.

'Close that door and don't come back till I ring.'

Ben closed the door, and his master, in much the same curt tone, said to Mary Ann, 'Sit down!'

Slowly she eased the big chair from under the table and wriggled herself on to its seat, only to find that even when she perched on its edge she was too far away from the table; so she got down again, pushed the chair further in and squeezed herself between it and the table and on to its seat again. But now, not a little to her consternation, she found she was much nearer . . . the Lord. She watched him place half a tomato on a slice of bacon which was already reposing on a piece of fried bread. This he had put on his side plate, and when he pushed it towards her she wanted to say in a very civil voice, 'No, thank you, I'm not hungry'; but what she did was to take the knife he handed her and cut the bread and bacon by holding it firmly with one hand, since there was no fork available, and despatching it without further quibble or hesitation.

'What do you drink? Tea or milk?'

'Tea.'

'Then get a cup. You'll find one in there.' He pointed to a china cabinet, and she struggled off the chair again and went to the cabinet, and opening the doors took out a cup. It was thin and felt so light in her hand that for a moment she stood staring at it before returning to the table with it.

'Where do you live?'

'Mulhattans' Hall.'

'Where is that?'

'In Burton Street. Off Walter Street.'

'How old are you?'

'Gone eight.'

'Are you the only child?'

'No. There's our Michael. . . . He's going to the Grammar School; he passed an exam.'

'Indeed.'

'He's going to be a great scholar and earn a lot of money.' She offered this information in an ordinary conversational tone; but this soon changed when she heard him say, 'That's impossible, he can't do both.' The words were muttered more to himself, but immediately she took them up.

'He will! His teacher says he will. You don't believe anything.'

The cessation of hostilities was forgotten; the fact that she had just partaken of a miracle in the form of half his breakfast was neither appreciated nor understood.

'You're just the spit of Sarah Flannagan!' she finished.

'Who, may I ask, is Sarah Flannagan? Do you want a piece of bread and marmalade?'

'No. No, I don't ... I mean, no, thank you. She's a girl lives opposite us. She goes to our school, and she's a big liar, and she never believes anything.'

'And I'm like her?' He helped himself to marmalade, while Mary Ann paused to reconsider her verdict, blinking at him the while.

'Well, you don't believe anything, do you? You don't believe about me da, and that's like her. It's a wonder she's not struck down dead the things she's said about me da.'

'What kind of things?'

'Well.' Mary Ann paused as if there was need to recollect. 'Well, she said me da drinks. Now would you believe that?' She leant a little towards him; and he leaned back in his chair and surveyed her.

'And you say she's lying?'

'Yes. She's a bigger liar than Tom Pepper.'

'You did say your name was Shaughnessy, didn't you?'

'Yes.' Mary Ann was quite emphatic about this.

'And your father is called ... Mike. Is that right?'

'Yes.'

'And he's a big man, with red hair?' He waved his hand round his own white head as he spoke.

'Yes, that's him. Do you know me da?'

He ignored her question and said, 'And you say he doesn't drink?'

She stared at him, unblinking. Then she said quietly, 'Yes.'

As his head moved down towards her, her body began to stiffen but she continued to look him defiantly in the eye.

'Do you mean to sit there and tell me that your father doesn't drink at all?'

She moved her bottom quickly back and forward on the seat until the leather began to squeak. Then she brought out, 'I do. And,' she continued, slipping off the seat, 'I don't want any more of your tea or your breakfast, for you're as like as two pins with her. You can ask Father Owen about me da. He'll tell you what a right fine man he is.' She bounced her head once at him with finality. Then turning on her heel she marched towards the door.

'Where are you going now?'

'I'm going home.' She threw this over her shoulder.

'Come here.'

Mary Ann found that she was forced to turn at the command, and when once again she was standing by the side of the chair she had just left, he said again, 'You say your father doesn't drink?'

'I've told you.'

'You're a Catholic, aren't you?'

'Yes.'

'And still you say your father doesn't drink? Be careful now.'

Mary Ann stared at him, and her answer did not come immediately. But when it did it was still quite firm. 'I do.'

'Would you swear on it?' Now he seemed to be towering over her, and there was an odd look on his lined face. It had shed its stiff, hard mask and had taken on an expression that could only be called excitement; it sat strangely upon him, and he looked like a man who was watching a race.

Mary Ann's eyes widened, stretching across her face until they seemed almost to encompass it. It was one thing to fight the whole world for something that you wanted to believe, but to be made to swear on it . . . that was another thing entirely; and to be reminded that she was a Catholic into the bargain made things a thousand times worse. The Holy Family, with hurt expressions, were on one side of her, purgatory, hell and damnation gaped widely on the other; but in front of her, blotting out them all, even the face of this terrifying old man, stood her da, looking as she saw him last night before she went to bed, a drawn, changed, different da. Her lips began to tremble and her nose to twitch, but her eyes met Mr. Lord's without flinching. 'I would swear on it,' she said.

There was a taut silence in the room; then it was split by a laugh, the strangest laugh that Mary Ann had ever heard. She watched Mr. Lord lean back in his chair, and his thin body seemed to crack each time a staccato sound escaped his lips. The sounds mounted, and when he pressed his hands to his side Mary Ann's concern for him brought her to his knee.

'Have you got a stitch?'

Her attitude and concern only aggravated the stitch, for his laughter mounted. Neither of them noticed Ben come into the room and it was not until he spoke, asking in an awed voice, 'Are you all right, sir?' that Mr. Lord, with a noticeable effort, took hold of himself. His laughter weakened and became spasmodic, but Ben's concern grew when his master, looking at him with streaming eyes, said, 'The greatest of these is loyalty.'

The old man looked at Mary Ann and there was fear in his eyes, and when he turned to his master once again Mr. Lord waved him away. 'Go on – go on,' he said; but as the old servant went again reluctantly out of the room his master's eyes followed him.

Mr. Lord had never considered before that he had been the recipient of loyalty for over forty years. He had taken Ben for granted. He had growled at and abused him, first because no other servant would live with him, then because of the state of the house, then just because it had become a habit. He had sacked him countless times; he had even stopped his money to make him go, but it had made no difference. For years he had seen Ben as an old nuisance who hung on because he wouldn't be able to get a job anywhere else. Ben was twenty-eight when he first came to work for him, and he knew everything there was to know about him. He had witnessed the madness of his marriage; he had seen its end; and as isolation had become his defence he had clung closer to him. Yet, it was strange, he had never before this morning looked upon Ben's service as loyalty. It had taken this child, who could lie with the innocence of an angel and the purpose of a priest, to show him just how much of the same loyalty had he himself been receiving all these years.

Mr. Lord wiped his eyes. But why should he have laughed? It was many a long year since his body had shaken with such laughter as this child had inspired. He looked at her through his swimming eyes. Her face was like a film flickering the thoughts of her mind across its surface; she imagined that she had only to stick to her guns and he would see her father as she saw him. If he hadn't known Mike Shaughnessy he would have, without doubt, believed every word she said. She did not look a bit like Red Mike, yet there was something of him there. Perhaps it was her tenacity – given an idea she would hang on to it until she died – that was him. If only he had the right ideas. But apparently, to him, they were right for he was willing to lose his job for them – yes, and to cause strikes through them. No, he must be fair to the man – he would have caused no strike in his yard; he was too much of an individualist; he could sway neither side completely for he pointed too blatantly to the rottenness of both. It was because his own conscience had been pricked by the man that he was so mad at him. Yet it was strange that all this big red-headed hulk wanted was to work on the land and have his family near him.

'Are you all right now?'

He nodded to her. 'Yes, yes, I'm all right.'

'I get like that when I go to the pictures and I see a comic, the stitch gets me in the side and I want to cry when I'm laughing ... it's awful. Will I pour you out another cup of tea?'

'Yes – can you?'

'Oh yes, I often do the tea at home. There.' She pushed a

cup towards him, and he lifted it and drank while he continued to look down at her.

'What are you going to do when you go back home this morning?' he asked.

Her eyes dropped from his, and she replied dully, 'Nothing.'

He handed the cup back to her and with the side of his finger he smoothed down his white moustache; then hesitantly, almost as if he wanted to find favour with her, he said, 'Will you have time then to take a little ride with me to ... to the farm?'

They looked at each other. The significance of the request took on a tangible form; it shone between them, blinding Mary Ann with its promise; it formed a fairy-like castle on a high mountain; and she was choked with its wonder. She could bear no more. She flung herself at his feet, her arms about his legs, and when he, making strange tut-tutting sounds, attempted to quieten her noisy sobs, her crying only increased. With gruff tenderness he coaxed her up, and when she leant against him it seemed the natural sequence that he should then lift her on to his knee.

He had in his time been kissed both passionately and falsely by women, but never had he been kissed by a child, never had he felt that ecstatic grip of thin arms about his neck. In this moment he would willingly have changed places with Mike Shaughnessy.

CHAPTER TEN

THE TRUTH, AND NOTHING BUT ...

IT had been a grand morning, a lovely morning. Mary Ann wanted it to go on for ever, but there was her ma and her da and the letter. Lovingly she touched the pocket in which the letter reposed and edging herself further towards the front of the car seat, she smiled up at Mr. Lord. 'Will you take me round by our school?'

'Where's that?'

'Not far from the church, you know. Round Dee Street.'

'Oh.'

'Do you think we might be able to have a dog and a cat?'

'I don't see why not.'

'Have you a dog?'

'No.'

'You should have, in a big house like that, because it would scare burglars.'

'Yes ... yes, you're quite right.'

'Haven't you anyone to tidy up for you besides him?'

A spasm passed over Mr. Lord's face, moving the wrinkled skin like small lapping waves on a ridge of sand, but he answered quite seriously, 'No, only him.'

Mary Ann shook her head. 'Me ma's the right one for tidying up.'

'Is she?'

'Yes. Our house is like a new pin. Look ... there's our

school. You see that second window along the top? That's our class.'

Mr. Lord bent his head and looked up at the window, saying. 'Yes. Ah yes, I see.' Then he added, 'Can I put you down here? Can you find your way home?'

'Yes. Why yes,' she laughed up at him.

He was funny. Find her way home indeed ... she could find her way all over Jarrow by herself.

It was at this point when Mr. Lord was about to apply his brakes that Mary Ann, peering through the windscreen, saw in the distance a group of children, five in number, and all well known to her. One head in particular was so familiar that she almost choked with excitement and actually nudged him. 'Look ... along there. See those girls? Can I get off there? Will you ride me along there?'

Mary Ann, thinking she detected a slight hesitancy in Mr. Lord's manner, added urgently, 'The long one, that's Sarah Flannagan.'

'Oh-h.'

The car moved on again, and Mary Ann, her eyes starting from her head with the force of her feelings volunteered the information, 'She's the one as I told you of. When I've been telling girls about our car and horses she's always spoilt it ... she never believes it.'

'Dear, dear, doesn't she?' said Mr. Lord.

'No. But I was only making on, you know. But still, she should have believed it, shouldn't she?'

'Of course. Of course.'

'Well, now she'll see. She'll get the shock of her life. It wouldn't be any use me telling her on Monday that I'd been for a ride with you in a car. She'd say I was loppy and wanted me head looking.'

'She would indeed.' Mr. Lord brought the car to a slow stop just where the group of girls stood on the pavement, and leaning across Mary Ann he opened the door. With a grateful sidelong smile at him she edged herself off the seat, gave a little jump and landed on the pavement, face to face with Sarah Flannagan.

That Sarah was surprised is an understatement. She goggled, her mouth as it fell open looking out of all proportion to her face. Mary Ann gazed up at her, long and steadily, before allowing her shining eyes to flicker over the rest of the group, two of whom had been listeners to the ... big house, cars and horses tale, which Sarah Flannagan had shattered that particular night in the school-yard. Now Mary Ann, addressing herself solely and pointedly to Sarah, said, 'I've been for a ride and I've had me breakfast in a great big house. Like a palace it is. And we're going to move into a fine grand cottage with a great lump of garden, and me da's going to be somebody and me ma'll have nice clothes.'

To give Sarah her due she did try to speak. Her lips formed the usual phrase, but soundlessly, and they only got as far as 'Oh you great big ...' for her eyes lifted to the old man in the car. She knew who he was, everybody in Jarrow knew who he was, and Mary Ann Shaughnessy had just stepped out of his car.

Mr. Lord watched the little play, and groping back and clutching at a faint spark of devilment from his youth, suddenly brought all eyes towards himself, including Mary Ann's, when he said with slow pomp and using her name for the first time, 'Where did you say you wanted to go for a ride tomorrow, Mary Ann?'

A message that could only be read by Mary Ann came from his eyes, and she answered it with one that was touched with love. She moved towards the car window, 'Oh, Whitley Bay.'

'Whitley Bay it is then. And what time will I come?'

'Come for me, in the car?'

The proposal was filled with such phantasy that even she didn't for the moment believe it was true.

'Of course.' Mr. Lord's voice had a touch of the old asperity about it, and this itself conveyed to all present the serious and truthful intent of his purpose.

'Oh.' On a surge of rising joy came an inspiration to Mary Ann, and after casting a glance about her at the amazed faces she swallowed hard and said, 'Would you call for me then after Mass, the ten o'clock, at the church door?'

The meeting place obviously was a surprise to Mr. Lord, and his brows contracted for a moment as he repeated, 'The church door?'

'Yes.'

It was evident that the church door did not meet with Mr. Lord's approval. The sound that came from him was akin to a groan, and Mary Ann, looking apprehensively, said in a small voice, 'Well, can you?'

He moved back in his seat pulling the car door closed as he did so. His expression looked to Mary Ann very like the one he was wearing before he'd had his breakfast.

'Good-bye,' she said softly.

'Good-bye,' said Mr. Lord.

Suddenly she knew she couldn't let him go like this. Reaching up, she peered over the lowered glass of the window and whispered, 'Are you vexed?'

For a moment he looked at her; then his eyes crinkled into a smile and his hand came out to her cheek, 'I'll be there.'

Until the car had passed from sight around the corner of the street Mary Ann did not move, and when she did it was to walk away with her chin in the air and without even a glance at or word to Sarah Flannagan and the girls. The ground was still shaking under her feet; she fully realized it had been touch and go about the church door; also that its accomplishment was a glory that wouldn't come her way twice. Tomorrow morning when all the school was coming out of church there would be the car to meet her. Sarah

Flannagan and all the lot of them, even the teachers would see her. The emotion was partly agony.

She had reached the corner of the street before she realized that not a solitary jeer had followed her, not even the usual gibe of 'Mary Ann, frying pan!' She turned round, and there they were where she had left them, standing like dummies. Unable to resist a parting shot she turned her back, lifted up her short skirt, and thrust her bottom out at them.

*　　*　　*

The voice of Fanny McBride rang up the staircase with the force of a sergeant-major on the barrack-square. She was holding on to the bottom banister with both hands as she cried once again, 'Mike! Mike! You, Lizzie – she's here, walking down the street as large as life.'

She had scarcely finished before Mike was descending the last flight of stairs towards her.

'Look for yourself.' She followed him to the door and called out over her shoulder, 'What did I tell you, Liz? I knew she would turn up. She's not the kind to go and tip herself in the river . . . not Mary Ann.'

Mary Ann walked up the steps towards her parents. Her eyes darted from one to the other. She spared no glance for Mrs. McBride or Miss Harper, or the Laveys who were now crowding the hallway, but the suppressed excitement about her made itself felt, and she asked in an airy tone, 'What's the matter, Ma?'

'Listen to her. What's the matter, Ma?' Fanny's laugh vibrated round the hall. 'Only half the town looking for you, polismen an' all.'

Mike and Lizzie both stood staring down on her as if they were finding it hard to believe the evidence of their eyes, and it was Mike who eventually spoke. 'Where've you been?' he asked.

Mary Ann did not at first reply, but looked up at her father. His voice was harsh and his face was harsh and he wasn't like her da at all. His face looked even worse than it had done last night, and his manner had the power to crush her gaiety and she replied meekly, 'In the country.'

'In the country ... well, I'll be damned!' Fanny slapped her thigh, and Lizzie, saying nothing, reached out and taking Mary Ann's hand led her through the little press and up the stairs.

Once in the room and the door closed, Lizzie suddenly sat down. It was as if her legs had been whipped from under her. She put her hand for a moment to her brow and covered her eyes, then softly she asked, 'Where've you been? I want the truth, mind.'

'In the country, Ma.'

'Why did you go out like that ... so early?'

Mary Ann looked from her mother to where Mike was standing glaring down at her, and she found she couldn't say. There wasn't very much time left, so she substituted, 'I wanted to get back soon but we went for a ride in the car.'

The room became so still that Mary Ann scraped her foot on the lino in order to make some familiar sound.

'Whose car? Who have you been with? Now no lies.' The tone of her father's voice wiped the remaining joy from the morning. It was if she had done something wrong ... and him saying 'no lies'. As if she told lies for herself — she told lies only to make things come right for him. Her lips trembled and her head drooped and she muttered 'Mr. Lord's.'

'Mr. Whose?'

'Lord's ... him who has the farm.'

Slowly Mike came to her. 'You went to Mr. Lord's? What for?'

'To tell him ... to tell him ...' Now she was sniffling and

Lizzie said, 'Sh! There now. Just tell us what happened and you won't get wrong.'

'I went to tell him what a . . . a grand man you were with . . . with horses and cows and things.'

For a brief moment Mike's eyes held Lizzie's; then he turned slowly towards the fire, and Lizzie, gathering the child to her said, 'Tell me what happened. How did you get into Mr. Lord's place?'

'I got through the barbed wire, and the old man let me in, and Mr. Lord give me half his breakfast. Then we went to see the cottage.' She lifted her head from her mother's breast and still sniffing continued, 'Oh it's a lovely cottage, Ma; he's given us the best one.'

As Mike swung round exclaiming, 'What did you say?' Lizzie pressed Mary Ann away from her, and holding her at arm's length demanded, 'What are you talking about, child?'

'The cottage that goes with the farm, Ma. He gave me a letter – here—' she pulled the letter from her pocket, and turning, handed it to Mike who took it and opened it without taking his eyes from her. When he did begin to read both Lizzie and Mary Ann watched him. Then he slowly lifted his head and silently contemplated Mary Ann. His head shaking with a slight bewildered movement, he handed the letter to Lizzie and went into the room, walking, Mary Ann thought to herself, as if he'd already had a few.

After a moment Lizzie's hands dropped into her lap and she too stared at Mary Ann in a bewildered fashion; then without any warning she began to cry, not a quiet easy crying, but a crying that was tinged with laughter and touched on hysteria. It brought Mike back to the kitchen and after only a moment's hesitation, during which his face worked convulsively, he went to her and gathered her into his arms and smothered her wild cries against his breast.

Mary Ann stood apart, watching. The emotions that were coursing through her were too tangled and complex for her to experience any one of them consciously; she could not put a name to the feeling of deflation their combined force created; she could not even think that her da holding her ma in his arms again portended nothing but good. One thing only was evident to her, everything had turned out quite differently from what she had imagined. Her news hadn't been greeted with open arms; she hadn't been hugged and kissed and told what a clever girl she was; instead, she had been accused of lying. Why, when she came to think of it, the only one who believed her was the Lord himself. He thought she was a clever girl; he had told her so when he put the letter into her hand. And because he realized she was a clever girl she had given him her entire confidence – she had related graphically just how Sarah Flannagan had banged her head against the wall because of what happened on Coronation Day, and he had laughed and laughed. She had even told him about how she went in the black dark for Mrs. McBride the night their Michael put his head in the gas oven. The more she told him the more he laughed and she knew he believed everything she said.

She had decided much earlier in the morning that she liked Mr. Lord. She had even decided to take him under her wing, for all he needed was a good laugh and his house tidying up and he'd be all right.

She watched her da lead her ma into the bedroom, and when the door closed on them she felt indeed alone. She stood irresolute for a moment; then with a flop she sat on a chair and was preparing herself to feel very misused when the outer door burst open and Michael appeared. He gave no welcome cry at the sight of her but in his brotherly fashion advanced towards her demanding, 'Where do you think you've been?'

She did not answer but looked up at him with a sidelong

glance fully calculated to aggravate his already harassed feelings.

'Where's me Ma and Da? The motor cops are looking for you.' He looked around the room. 'Where's me Ma?'

Still Mary Ann said no word, and her air of superiority, which at any time had the power to annoy him, infuriated him now. Without further words he stretched both hands out to grab her, but like lightning she slipped beneath them and, still without speaking, she aimed one well-cobbled toecap at his shin.

On his cry of real pain the morning suddenly balanced itself again and her depression lifted. Life was normal, the world was full of magic, she was cleverer than their Michael even if he was going to the Grammar School; they had a cottage in the country, her ma and her da weren't going to leave each other . . . and there was Mr. Lord. And tomorrow morning he'd be at the church waiting for her for all the world to see.

Michael, hopping on one leg, cried, 'For two pins I'd . . .' and she answered pertly, 'Oh, would you? Well wait a minute and I'll get them for you.'

'Mary Ann.' On her name being called softly from the bedroom door, she swung round and there stood her da. They looked at each other for a moment before he held out his arms to her and almost in one leap she was in them, hugging and being hugged with such intensity that even Sunday morning became blotted out.

*   *   *

Now came the Elevation of the Host. Mary Ann knelt with bowed head and beat her narrow chest with clenched fist as each tinkle of the bell came from the altar and she murmured with every thump, 'Lord be merciful to me, a sinner; Lord be merciful to me, a sinner.' She drew a deep breath as she raised her head after the last tinkle. Ah, that was over. There wasn't much more now. Soon John Finlay would carry the big book from one side of the altar to the other and then Father Owen would say 'Our Father' and 'Hail Mary' and a little bit more, and then. . . . The excitement began to tear round inside her again, almost making her feel sick. Eeh, she mustn't be sick. She had been sick last night, but she hadn't minded for both her ma and her da had held her head, and it wasn't because she had eaten any sweets or anything or had had anything fancy for her tea. She had felt the sickness coming on in the afternoon while she waited for her da to come back. He had gone out all dressed up to see Mr. Lord and he hadn't returned till nearly seven o'clock, but for once her ma hadn't looked worried. She had looked quiet and calm – she had looked like that since she had unpacked their clothes – and her da had looked quiet too. She remembered at dinner time they had all sat round a makeshift meal, and Mrs. McBride had come up and had cried, 'Lord, ye're as quiet as a bunch of survivors from a wreck,' and her da had said in an odd way, 'Just as quiet, Fanny.' And when he came back from Mr. Lord's he was still quiet and he wasn't quite himself, but he wasn't sick or anything. Oh no, for she knew he hadn't touched a drop. But he seemed as if he must have her near him; and after she was sick he had even washed her himself and put her to bed. Oh, it had been a grand week-end, a lovely week-end. And it wasn't over. Oh no, not by a long time – there was all today.

Oh, if Father Owen would only put a move on . . . Eeh, what was she saying? After all the Holy Family had done for her, and . . . She tut-tutted to herself. Would you believe it, she had never even thanked them properly. She turned her face to the side altar and found to her surprise that as she had nothing at the moment to ask of them she was a little at a loss for words. Hesitatingly she began, 'Dear Blessed Holy Family, thank you for all you have done for me, for getting me da a job and for the cottage.' It all sounded so inadequate, sort of mean. She felt that something was expected of her, some present of some sort. Well, she'd light a candle the morrer – she just couldn't spare the time this morning. The mean feeling persisted and she thought, 'I know what ... I know what'll please them more than anything.' She unlaced her fingers and put her hands finger-tip to finger-tip as she usually did when dealing with matters of import. 'Dear Holy Family. I promise you faithfully, so help me, that I'll never tell another lie. May I be struck down dead if I do.' There, she felt better, and the Holy Family looked very pleased, but it still felt funny not having anything to ask them to do. She was about to turn her attention back to the main altar where John Finlay was now moving the book when she suddenly thought of her grannie. Now there was something they could do to get on with. Solemnly and fluently now she beseeched them, 'Dear Holy Family, could you do something about me grannie to stop her from coming out to our cottage? Could you give her a bad leg or something? You needn't kill her off, just stop her. In the name of the Father, Son, Holy Ghost, Amen.'

She got that in just in time to give the responses with the rest of the children to the priest saying the first half of the 'Our Father.' On the third 'Hail Mary' her responses were loud and clear and very definite, as if she herself had some proprietary right in their saying ... 'Holy Mary – Mother of God – pray for us sinners – now and at the hour of our death – Ah-men.'

Ah ... there, it was over. Father Owen had not disappeared through the vestry door before she was on her feet.

'Sit down and wait until the class is out.' A hand on her shoulder and the hissed command from Miss Johnson brought her bottom abruptly into contact with the hard seat.

Oh, Miss Johnson! She had eyes like a gimlet. Oh dear!

Bust! Now as like as not she'd keep her back till the very last.

Which was exactly what Miss Johnson did. Row after row of children swarmed methodically into the aisle. With noisy caution they kicked against the wooden kneelers, gasped audibly as they genuflected towards the altar, and invariably scraped their feet on the heating grids.

Mary Ann kept her eyes riveted on Miss Johnson's back, but Miss Johnson seemed to have entirely forgotten Mary Ann's presence. She was standing six rows away and apparently in another world.

Oh the beast . . . oh she was awful. Mary Ann wriggled on her seat as if she were already on that gridiron so often prophesied by her grannie. Everybody would be gone home. Perhaps even Mr. Lord would think she'd gone, and he'd go away. There was no fear strong enough to keep her in her seat; she rose to her feet and, moving quietly into the aisle, genuflected and bowed her head to the altar, only to lift it to Miss Johnson's legs which she surmised had been whipped in front of her by lightning, or the devil.

'I thought I told you to wait until the church emptied?'

You don't argue with a teacher or Mary Ann would have said, 'You said wait until the class had gone, which is quite a different thing from waiting until the church was empty.'

Perhaps the swish of Father Owen's gown had some influence on Miss Johnson's censure, for she murmured softly, 'Go on now; but come to me in the morning.'

Without a word Mary Ann turned away, and it was only with the greatest restraint that she stopped herself from running up the aisle – or was it the fact that she was 'twixt the devil and the deep sea, with Miss Johnson behind her and Father Owen in front?

Father Owen paused before going out into the porch and patted the heads of self-conscious philanthropists as she or he made a great show of putting a penny into the poor box or lighting a candle to their favourite saint. Mary Ann did neither, but she was going past him, actually without looking at him and on the verge of a run now, when his hand descended on her head.

'What have you been up to?' he whispered.

'Nothing, Father.'

'You were kept in.'

'Yes, Father, 'cause I wanted to get out quick.'

A twinkle in his eye softened the harshness of his words. 'Out quick? away from God as quickly as you can?'

'No, Father. But you see, it's a special morning.'

Oh dear, dear. Wouldn't he take his hand off her head? She glanced with evident longing towards the door. 'What's extra special about it?'

'Mr. Lord – he's come to take me for a ride . . . I was going to come and tell you last night but I was sick and vomited all over the place.'

'Mr. Lord?' The pressure on her head became heavier and her hat was hurting her ears. The priest bent nearer to her. 'What were you saying about Mr. Lord?'

'He's given me da a job and a fine cottage. I prayed to the Holy Family and they told me to go and have a talk with him, just like you said yourself, Father. Oh Father, can I go now?'

He took his hand from her head but said, 'Wait a minute. When did you talk to him?'

'Yesterday morning, Father. I got up early and crawled through the barbed wire and knocked on his door.'

Father Owen straightened up. He could not step back for he was already against the wall, but he drew his chin in and half closed his eyes as if to focus her better, then he began to chuckle.

Mary Ann could not go without his word, but she moved from one foot to the other just to show him the extent of her need to hurry. But he only continued to chuckle. 'Where is he going to meet you?'

'Outside, Father, just outside—' she pointed to the door and moved a step towards it, trying to draw him with her.

'Did you ask him to meet you outside here?'

'Yes, Father.'

He continued to stare at her, but he remained where he was. He knew exactly why she had requested the car to be brought to the church just after Mass but he could not for the life of him imagine what form her persuasion had taken to make Peter Lord agree to bringing it. His head wagged. 'Well, well.' And he had given Mike the job. Again 'Well, well.' And all through this little mite's tongue. . . . Nothing she would do or say would ever surprise him.

But here Father Owen was wrong.

'Will you come and see, Father, or else he'll be away?'

'No. No, Mary Ann . . . you run along.'

This was her hour. He knew his presence out on the street would only deflect some of the children's attention from her and he guessed he'd be the last person Peter Lord would wish to see this morning. No, he'd stay where he was.

'I'll come and tell you all about it the morrer. Good-bye, Father.'

She was gone; and after waiting a few seconds Father Owen's good intentions were also gone. Cautiously he went into the porch and towards the main doorway.

The crowd that awaited Mary Ann was somewhat disappointing. There weren't more than twenty-five altogether. . . . It was that beastly Miss Johnson's fault. They had all gone home; and the car wasn't right opposite the church door either, but some way along the street.

However, the number of the crowd did not matter so much, it was the quality of it that counted. And the quality to her was of the best, for it consisted of most of her class and, pleasure upon pleasure, Sarah Flannagan.

The car was facing her and as she ran towards it holding on to her hat with one hand she waved to the grim face behind the wheel with the other, and it was no imagination on her part that the face relaxed into a smile and a hand was raised in response to her salute.

'Get by!' Mary Ann directed this command to Sarah Flannagan who was standing on the pavement well to the side of the car door. In fact, all the children had kept a respectful distance from the car. Sarah was no more in Mary Ann's way than were two or three of the other children, and she did not, as some of the others did, shuffle a few steps to the side, but she stood her ground. 'Get by yersel,' she said.

Mary Ann got by. She walked round her enemy with her lips and her nose pursed and eye to eye with her, for Sarah slowly pivoted in the same direction.

As Mary Ann reached the car door it opened, but she gave no word of greeting to Mr. Lord, only smiled warmly at him before ducking beneath his outstretched arm to sit herself with dignity on the edge of the seat. The door banged and there was a soft purr, then from the open window she faced the little crowd of children, now gathered closer about the car; but her eyes rested only on one, and to Sarah she addressed herself.

'Now you see who's a liar, Sarah Flannagan. You wouldn't believe about our house and the cars and the horses, would you? Well, we're going into our new house the morrer, and there's four horses, and me da's got a right fine job, better than your da will ever have, 'cause he's a drunken no-good and' – her voice rose to a shrill pipe and all her dignity vanished – 'if you dare to call me a liar again you won't half catch it, because this . . .' she cried finally, sticking her head out of the window now and jerking her thumb over her shoulder, 'is me Granda!'

There was a shocked silence in Heaven, while down in the

church porch Father Owen bent his head and covered his face with one hand.

* * *

'There you go — I tell you it did happen. Ooh! you'll believe nothing – it's like Sarah Flannagan you are.'

OUR KATE by CATHERINE COOKSON

An Autobiography

The *Our Kate* of the title is not Catherine Cookson, but her mother, around whom the autobiography revolves. She is presented with all her faults, yet despite these, Kate comes out as a warm and lovable human figure. And against this central character, we see the child Catherine going to 'the pawn', fetching the beer, and collecting driftwood from the river for the family struggle through an era when work was scarce and social security non-existent.

So *Our Kate* is a story of a person and a period. It is an honest statement about living with hardship and poverty, seen through the eyes of a highly sensitive child and woman, whose zest for life and unquenchable sense of humour won through to make Catherine Cookson the warm, engaging and *human* writer she is today.

0 552 11676 9   £1.25

THE INVITATION by CATHERINE COOKSON

When the Gallachers received an invitation from the Duke of Moorshire to attend his musical evening. Maggie was overwhelmed. Naturally, she did not see the invitation as the rock on which she was to perish; nor was she prepared for the reactions of her family. Her son Paul, daughter Elizabeth and daughter-in-law Arlette were as delighted as she was but the effect on Sam, Arlette's husband, was to bring his smouldering hate of his mother to flashpoint. Maggie herself, however, was to be prime mover of the downfall of the family she loved too dearly . . .

0 552 11260 7   £1.50

CATHERINE COOKSON NOVELS
IN CORGI

WHILE EVERY EFFORT IS MADE TO KEEP PRICES LOW, IT IS SOMETIMES
NECESSARY TO INCREASE PRICES AT SHORT NOTICE. CORGI BOOKS
RESERVE THE RIGHT TO SHOW AND CHARGE NEW RETAIL PRICES ON
COVERS WHICH MAY DIFFER FROM THOSE ADVERTISED IN THE TEXT
OR ELSEWHERE.

THE PRICES SHOWN BELOW WERE CORRECT AT THE TIME OF GOING TO
PRESS (APRIL '81)

☐ 11350 6	THE MAN WHO CRIED	£1.25
☐ 11160 0	THE CINDER PATH	£1.25
☐ 10916 9	THE GIRL	£1.75
☐ 11202 X	THE TIDE OF LIFE	£1.95
☐ 11374 3	THE GAMBLING MAN	£1.50
☐ 11204 6	FANNY MCBRIDE	£1.25
☐ 11261 5	THE INVISIBLE CORD	£1.75
☐ 11571 1	THE MALLEN LITTER	£1.50
☐ 11570 3	THE MALLEN GIRL	£1.50
☐ 11569 X	THE MALLEN STREAK	£1.50
☐ 11677 7	ROONEY	£1.25
☐ 11391 3	PURE AS THE LILY	£1.50
☐ 11676 9	OUR KATE	£1.25
☐ 11674 2	FEATHERS IN THE FIRE	£1.50
☐ 11203 8	THE DWELLING PLACE	£1.95
☐ 11260 7	THE INVITATION	£1.50
☐ 11365 4	THE NICE BLOKE	£1.35
☐ 11675 0	THE GLASS VIRGIN	£1.75
☐ 11366 2	THE BLIND MILLER	£1.50
☐ 11434 0	THE MENAGERIE	£1.25
☐ 11367 0	COLOUR BLIND	£1.50
☐ 11448 0	THE UNBAITED TRAP	£1.25
☐ 11335 2	KATIE MULHOLLAND	£1.95
☐ 11447 2	THE LONG CORRIDOR	95p
☐ 11449 9	MAGGIE ROWAN	£1.50
☐ 11368 9	THE FIFTEEN STREETS	£1.25

☐ 11336 0	FENWICK HOUSES	£1.25
☐ 11369 7	THE ROUND TOWER	£1.50
☐ 11370 0	KATE HANNIGAN	£1.25
☐ 08822 6	THE LORD AND MARY ANN	£1.00
☐ 08823 4	THE DEVIL AND MARY ANN	£1.00
☐ 09074 3	LOVE AND MARY ANN	£1.25
☐ 09075 1	LIFE AND MARY ANN	£1.25
☐ 09076 X	MARRIAGE AND MARY ANN	£1.00
☐ 09254 1	MARY ANN'S ANGELS	£1.00
☐ 09397 1	MARY ANN AND BILL	£1.00

Writing as Catherine Marchant

☐ 11521 5	THE IRON FACADE	£1.25
☐ 11205 4	THE SLOW AWAKENING	£1.50
☐ 11373 5	MISS MARTHA MARY CRAWFORD	£1.50
☐ 11371 9	THE FEN TIGER	£1.25
☐ 11337 9	HERITAGE OF FOLLY	£1.35
☐ 11372 7	HOUSE OF MEN	£1.25

All these books are available at your bookshop or newsagent, or can be ordered direct from the publisher. Just tick the titles you want and fill in the form below.

CORGI BOOKS, Cash Sales Department, P.O. Box 11, Falmouth, Cornwall.

Please send cheque or postal order, no currency.

Please allow cost of book(s) plus the following for postage and packing.

U.K. CUSTOMERS. 40p for the first book, 18p for the second book and 13p for each additional book ordered, to a maximum charge of £1.49.

B.F.P.O. & EIRE. Please allow 40p for the first book, 18p for the second book plus 13p per copy for the next three books, thereafter 7p per book.

OVERSEAS CUSTOMERS. Please allow 60p for the first book plus 18p per copy for each additional book.

NAME (block letters) ....

ADDRESS ....

(APRIL 1981) ....